A True Map of the City

Lost in Dystopia

J GUENTHER

🝮 Wyzard Hill Press 🝮

A TRUE MAP OF THE CITY

Copyright © 2018 by J Guenther.

Published by Wyzard Hill Press

Palos Verdes, California

No parts of this publication may be reproduced, stored in a retrieval system, or transmitted in any form or by any means, electronic, mechanical, photocopying, recording, or otherwise, without the prior written permission of the copyright owner.

This book is sold subject to the condition that it shall not, by way of trade or otherwise, be lent, resold, hired out, or otherwise circulated without the publisher's prior consent in any form of binding or cover other than that in which it is published and without a similar condition including this condition being imposed on the subsequent purchaser. Under no circumstances may any part of this book be photocopied for resale.

This is a work of fiction. Any similarity between the characters and situations within its pages and places or persons, living or dead, is unintentional and co-incidental.

For information contact:
https://JGuentherAuthor.WordPress.com

Book and Cover design by J Guenther. Typeset in 11 pt Crimson Text Semibold, designed by Sebastian Kosch

Printed in the United States of America
ISBN: 978-0-9974503-2-3
First Edition: October 2018

10 9 8 7 6 5 4 3 2 1

CC0 public domain photo by Martin Vorel via libreshot.com

Also by J Guenther

Fiction

Sail Away on My Silver Dream, World Nouveau Books, 2012 *

In the Mouth of the Lion, Wyzard Hill Press, 2013

Non-Fiction

The Fuehrer Recognition Kit, Wyzard Hill press, 2016

* Praise for Sail Away on My Silver Dream

A fanciful book that deals with some of today's real problems. I recommend it highly. A very enjoyable read. – Jean Shriver

This book is for anyone dealing with alcoholism, domestic violence and loss. Very realistic. – Mary Jo Hazard, MFT

Guenther's sensitive portrayal of two kids who find their way through difficult times by sailing to exotic, faraway places aboard their imaginary sailboat, the Silver Dream, is a story that will be enjoyed by young readers, and treasured by readers of all ages. – Dave Kenney.

Dedications

To my teachers:

Gibson Reaves, Richard Condon, Dr. Julia McCorkle, Jeff Hoppenstand, Edith Battles, Anne Lowenkopf, Glad Esther Mitchell, Bill Barnett.

Chapter One

It was the dwarf who most upset me. I'd barely arrived in Deres-Thorm on my way to a conference essential to my career. My claustrophobia in full sway, I stumbled from the cramped railway compartment, desperate to reach the open spaces of the terminal, despite the latter's unpleasant odour of locomotive oil and smoke. The porter deposited my luggage on the platform, silently extracted a gratuity from me, and scurried away, leaving me to manoeuvre my five suitcases to the customs counter however I could.

There was a long queue, so I arranged my bags around me and waited, exhausted from the journey and weary from lack of sleep. I wanted to sit on one of my larger suitcases, but thought that might seem undignified.

That was when the dwarf approached. A misshapen creature, he did a handstand directly in front of me. I tried to ignore him. He stood, smiled at me, and drew three greengages from a pocket. He held them towards me.

I'd been told that more or less everyone spoke Anglic in Deres-Thorm. "No, thank you," I said, but to be on the safe side, added the Deresthok equivalent, "*Splatka nin.*"

A TRUE MAP OF THE CITY

The dwarf, however, paid no attention and immediately began to juggle the greengages. Higher and higher they went, the dwarf grinning all the while. He vaguely repelled me, and I looked away in time to see the two largest (and most important) of my suitcases being carried off by a swarthy man. I yelled "Stop! Thief!" and ran after him, abandoning my other bags with utmost anxiety.

Propelled by the vestiges of my criquét prowess acquired while captain of my thirteen at school, I closed rapidly on the thief. I had almost caught him when he suddenly released both bags directly in my path. By the time I had stumbled, fallen, and righted myself, the man was far away. If I were a person who is accustomed to profanity, I would certainly have employed it.

I retrieved the bags and returned to the customs counter. As I'd feared, my other bags had vanished. I became agitated, but two of the people in the queue said something I didn't understand and pointed towards the far end of the terminal, where I saw the dwarf, the three missing bags balanced upon his head, attempting to flee from several dark-clad men. Had I been of a humourous nature, and had those not been my own bags, I would possibly have been amused at the sight of the overly-encumbered dwarf, his little legs almost a blur beneath him.

A minute later, transport officials dragged the dwarf away in manacles and restored my bags to me. I thanked the strangers who had aided me, and I returned to the queue, where others had saved my place.

But my ordeal had not ended. Upon reaching the customs table, I presented my papers. A glowering official grabbed them, examined them, and growled, "*¿Neezgo twa guzen damisk?*" He stared at me, waiting for a response.

I had studied Deresthok for over six months at our company offices. The tutor had assured me that I was completely fluent in the vocabulary, which was complex, and in the grammar, which was even more so. Yet now I had not a single clue as to the meaning of any word the man had spoken to me. I grew flustered and blurted out, "*Shtandrek nuss*," then added in Anglic, "I don't understand." My stomach began its usual gymnastics for this sort of situation. In my haste, I'd used the impolite Deresthok form of "not."

"*¿Neezgo twa guzen damisk!*" the official repeated, a bit louder, shaking my papers.

"*Shtandrek nin.*" I said, shrugging politely.

He frowned at me. I had visions of being dragged away in manacles like the dwarf, for whom I'd acquired a sudden, though illogical, sympathy.

"*E sokkt no fegrosty,*" interjected a roughly dressed man behind me. The words were unfamiliar, but in context, I took this to mean, "He say no understand." The man took off his battered straw hat, moved closer to the counter, and bowed deeply, not rising until the official looked at him and said:

"*Damisk logo bernta desen neezgoi tui.*"

I recognized one word this time, *logo*. "Logo" is Deresthok for bumpkin. I thought for a second that the customs man was rudely addressing the chap with the bucolic hat, but a thumb thrust in my direction by the official made it clear whom he meant.

The farmer, if that's what he was, turned to me and, gesturing, spoke in perfectly intelligible Deresthok, saying: "He wants to know why you are here."

I answered in kind. "I am here for business conference."

He faced the official and rattled off a string of words that I couldn't follow. It suddenly struck me what was happening. My tutor had once, in passing, mentioned that Deresthia had two very different dialects, one used in the capital and one used mostly by farmers, laborers, and other simple people in the outlying areas. The tutor had told me this, but all the while he had evidently, for some unknown

A TRUE MAP OF THE CITY

reason, been teaching me the countryside dialect, instead of the metropolitan version I'd requested. I'd been bamboozled.

I explained this to my interpreter, who smiled and told the official, who, to my discomfort, laughed until tears rolled down his cheeks. He then turned and told all his colleagues, as well. My embarrassment as they joined in raucous laughter was exceeded only by my dismay that my carefully devised plan to impress all the conference attendees with my fluent Deresthok was ruined. I would have to give my lengthy opening speech in Anglic or be regarded as a rustic oaf.

The three of us managed to exchange the necessary information. The official stamped my papers, handed them back to me, and said, "*Vilkom Deresthia.*"

Out of gratitude, I offered my farmer-interpreter a fifty malapek note, but he seemed reluctant to take it. The customs official, however, without hesitation, reached across the counter and plucked the note from my fingers, then shooed both of us away. The farmer was not displeased with this arrangement and gave me a little grin as we parted. The official had apparently forgotten to inspect his papers.

I, for my part, had forgotten to enquire about a map. The travel agency, Herrs Lazar und Budicroux, had had no street maps of the city of Deres-Thorm, but had promised me one upon my arrival. My tutor had warned me more than once not to explore the great city without a map, and I'd intended to obtain one at the train station.

Unaware of this oversight, with the aid of a porter, I immediately sought a steam-powered taxicab to Hotel Indigo, the finest lodging in Deres-Thorm, or so I had been assured by Lazar und Budicroux.

§☙

My exhaustion did not permit me to appreciate the antique splendour of my hotel. I vaguely noticed deep, red carpeting and oversize potted palms in the lobby and a gigantic, dusty crystal chandelier above the front desk. I was the only guest present, which I assumed was due to the late hour.

When I presented my passport and visa to the desk clerk, he studied them at length. I felt a strong urge to close my weary eyes, drop my head to the counter, and rest. I did not, of course. The clerk would surely have thought me unrefined or, perhaps, a bit barmy.

As I stood there, waiting patiently, a small black spider plopped from the chandelier overhead onto the open ledger. I imagined for a moment that I had dreamt this.

The clerk put down my papers, and, squashing the spider with a fingertip, referred to the ledger. After a long pause, he stared at me over his spectacles.

"You have reserwation, *Zemor*..." He glanced over at the visa. "... Zemor Blessisname?"

"Yes, but the name is Blassingame, Horus Blassingame."

He pushed his spectacles back up his nose and peered down at the ledger. "We have no reserwation in name of Blassing ... Blassingame, you did say?"

"Yes, Blassingame." I spelt the name out for the man, hoping that my irritation was not apparent.

He leafed to and fro through the ledger, comparing the name on my visa with his list of reservations. "No," he said at last. "No Blassingame."

"Obviously a mistake has been made," I replied.

"Obwiously," he said, staring at me coldly. It was clear who he thought had made the mistake.

"Let me talk to the manager," I demanded.

"That will not do you good. Manager will just look at ledger, as I haff already done." He gestured at the book with both hands.

"Haven't you any rooms at all?" I asked.

The man shook his head. "Not without reserwation."

"Could I see your reservation ledger?"

His eyebrows rose. "See our reserwation ledger?"

"Yes, the ledger." I pointed.

He shrugged and swiveled the book around to let me read it. I ran my finger up and down the pages and soon encountered: 'Mr. Horace Plastingane, of Dinium, Albion.'

"Here it is," I said. "It's been misspelt."

The clerk spun the ledger and put his bespectacled nose close to the page. "This is not you. This is man named Plastingane."

My perturbation threatened to cause me to lose my temper. "No, no!" I said. "That is someone's feeble attempt to spell Blassingame! That is my reservation! It's got the right city, even."

"Is got wrong name, eefen."

"Well, has this 'Horace Plastingane' shown up? Where is he?" I waved a hand at the empty lobby.

The man shrugged and scratched his head, staring at the book. "He has obwiously not signed in yet. Maybe is late."

"No, he's not late; there's no train that arrives after mine. He's me!"

The clerk reluctantly let me sign the book. He then returned my "wisa," but took my passport, as is the practice in these countries. He rang the bell three times, and a trio of bellboys appeared and gathered up my luggage. As we started away from the desk, the clerk said, "Mr. Blassingame, one moment."

¿*What now,* I thought.

He handed me a large folded document of some sort. The paper was very stiff. *A map!* It was only then that I realized that, with all the fuss at the terminal, I'd totally forgotten to purchase one.

I thanked the clerk profusely and went away with the bellboys.

I had now been awake for forty hours and was dreaming on my feet, seeing visions of an expanse of clean white sheets, a soft pillow, blankets, and sweet sleep. I remember following the silent luggage boys down a corridor, then up, up, up in a swaying lift. Fortunately, the lift was of the open cage style, and didn't stimulate my claustrophobia much.

The lift chattered to a halt, and we got out and walked down more hallways. As we rounded each corner, I thought: *here it is, here in this hallway is my room at last. The lead boy will soon turn and put a key into one of these locks, and I'll be seconds away from sleep.* But after each corner, we walked an entire corridor, turned still another corner, where I saw more doors and empty red carpeting stretching out before us in silence.

Just as I was beginning to wonder if I'd already fallen asleep and was dreaming this nightmarish journey, the parade came to such a sudden halt that I ran into the last boy. The others caught me and kept me from falling. They looked at me with sudden smiles that vanished just as quickly. "Sorry," I told the boy. "Sleepy. *Zvaynu.*"

"*Shwayna,*" he corrected.

Ahead of us, a door was open; someone ushered me towards it. A single lamp glowing just inside the doorway lit the dull red carpeting of the room. I entered, searched for a bed in the shadows, found it. I don't remember the boys setting down the luggage and leaving. I don't remember tipping the lead boy, either, but I must have. I recall only the faded brocade bedspread coming towards me as I fell, face first, atop the bed, then bounced only once on the tightly-sprung mattress before oblivion took me.

Chapter Two

Morning was broken by a deep and mournful howl that seemed to fill the entire world. Terrified, I rolled off the bed, staggered to the window, and jerked the curtains aside, fully expecting a vision of planetary doom. But no blood-red moon or plutonic gods hurtled earthward from the sky. Instead, far beneath my window, barely visible in the faint light of dawn, stood row after row of puce-robed rogonists atop the yellow brick buildings along the avenue. The hideous cacophony was the sound of their horns, the great, brazen rogonhorns of Deres-Thorm.

I'd read of these horns in the guidebook, but had erroneously filed them mentally under musical instruments. I'd had no idea how awful the sound was. Now, it went on and on, new horns picking up the monotonous drone as others faded.

After a minute or more of this dirge, I grew sleepy again. I was quite ready for the rogonists to cease blowing, but the din continued. *This is sadistic*, I thought, yawning. *Is this their insane idea of greeting the dawn? Or is their intent to scare it back whence it came? What purpose does this serve, except to exercise the rogonists' lungs? None.* I no longer considered these implements musical in any sense, merely traditional noisemakers to annoy people who needed sleep, and only incidentally to celebrate morning's arrival. But I took due note of the sun rising through the fog beyond the faraway end of an avenue, and considered it greeted to my satisfaction. I visited the uncomfortably tiny loo, and returned to bed.

I awoke late, much later than I'd planned. My watch said it was almost 10 a.m. Fortunately, my vital meeting wasn't until 3 p.m., so I had plenty of time. But even the idea of being late made my stomach turn a somersault.

According to a notice in Anglic on the telephone stand, the hotel served a continental breakfast until the "third hour." I'd read enough about Deresthia to know that "the third hour" meant neither 3 a.m. nor 3 p.m. It meant three hours after dawn, or, in our reckoning, about 9 a.m., give or take a bit, depending on the season. I was therefore late for breakfast and early for lunch, which was served "from the sixth hour until the eighth hour." The notice also stated: "Food service of room possible among these hours."

I picked up the listening cone of the telephone, an ancient instrument of brass, wood, and hard black plastic of some sort, possibly the very earliest sort. There was no dial tone. I clicked the dual hooks, but nothing happened. I stood there, still in a blur from the previous day's travel, wondering whether there were restaurants nearby, when I heard breathy sounds and a voice:

"Hurrrr yootoo dehumeus ur view?"

These words were not in my lexicon of rural Deresthok phrases, and at first I took them to mean something or other in the city dialect. "¿Is it possible to get some room service," I asked in Anglic, ignoring what I'd heard.

There was more breathing, but nothing was said for a while. "Momen police," the voice said at last. I understood this, even in my stupor. The operator was looking for someone who spoke Anglic. Or, perhaps, given the likely premise that the speaker imagined he was speaking Anglic, someone who understood it. It was more than a "momen" before a new voice announced:

9

A TRUE MAP OF THE CITY

"Hurrrr yootoo dehumeus ur view?"

"I'd like to order breakfast." The phone went silent. Then I heard a faint sound like someone trying to speak with a pillow over his head. I couldn't understand even a single word he was saying. Another muffled voice (the first one?) joined in. The voices went back and forth for a while, then a third could be heard, similarly faint, but more authoritative. After several rounds of this conversation, a new party spoke clearly into the phone:

"Hurrrr yootoo dehumeus ur view?"

"Never mind." I hung up the phone and stalked about the room, opening cupboards and drawers. There was nothing in the nightstand except the obligatory pristine copy of the big grey book known as *"The Deresthian Book of Obeisance."* The latter, I'd been told by my tutor, consisted of a compilation of dozens upon dozens of Deresthian bureaucratic regulations translated into horrid Anglic in the form of wretched poetry. I opened the book, validated my tutor's low opinion, and slammed it shut, all within seven seconds.

Having run out of places to explore, I opened the door and stepped into the corridor. There was no one out there. Across the hall was another room, its door a wooden rectangle, featureless except for tarnished brass room number, doorknob, and keyhole escutcheon.

The doors were all shut. Not the slightest sound emanated from behind any of them. There were no shoes left in the corridor for the hotel bootblack to attend to, nor any empty room service breakfast trays. For all I knew, I was the only guest in this corridor, or in the entire hotel, for that matter.

I'd had no supper and was growing ravenous. I refreshed myself in the loo and changed. When done, I grabbed up my room key from the lamp stand by the door. At the last second, I remembered my map. I found it on the floor beside the bed and opened it by the window to see if any restaurants were shown.

But no. It was not a map. It was a history of Deresthia. In very fine print. Every leader of the government, from Boogdar the First to the present day, was described in glowing terms, a veritable genius, a saint, a wit, a philanthropist, every man jack of them. I threw the useless pamphlet on the bed and left the room, making sure my copy of *Deresthia on Fifty Malapeks a Day* was in my coat pocket. In that guidebook was a small map of the entirety of Deresthia, but none of its capital, Deres-Thorm, unfortunately.

I hunted for the lift. It took some time for me to realize I couldn't recall which way I'd come the previous evening. Ultimately, I succeeded in finding a staircase, which I descended.

My legs ached by the time I reached the bottom, where the stairs landed in a deserted service area of some sort, obviously not intended for guests. The floors were dirty, greenish mottled linoleum, worn through to the floorboards in places. Graffiti in the native tongue speckled the walls, some scratched, some in pencil, all incomprehensible to me, save one. "The Cult Soars," it read in Anglic.

A curling, fly-specked calendar from eleven years previous hung on one wall. Beside it stood a carelessly painted window that perhaps decades ago had overlooked an alley. Now there was hotel on both sides of the window, so it merely looked from one grubby service corridor into another. It was very depressing.

It took me several minutes to find my way from this maze of hallways into the hotel proper. I was happy to see carpeting again. I followed it and kept turning into the widest corridor whenever there was a choice.

Eventually, I found myself in the lobby. There was no one there, either. I considered leaving my key on the unattended desk, but grew nervous at the idea of being separated from it. I turned towards the front door and started away, feeling guilty.

"Your key, Zemor!" a voice said.

I turned. There was now a man, small and swarthy, leaning against the counter, his relaxed posture indicating that he'd been there for some time. If not, where had he come from? There were no doors near the front desk. I was sure he had not been there as I walked past, just seconds before. I went back and handed him the key, then started away as he hung it on one of the numbered hooks on the wall behind him. It was only then that I remembered the map promised by Lazar und Budicroux. I turned again and said, "¿Do you perhaps..."

There was no one there. The man was just as absent as the first time I passed the desk. I went outside, mapless. I didn't intend to go far, so I didn't feel anxious, merely piqued.

Unlike the interior of Hotel Indigo, this part of the city was visibly populated. Most people walked or rode pedal vehicles of two, three, or four wheels. A few women rode in the traditional sedan chairs, mostly open, carried by four sturdy young men. I knew enough of the local customs not to stare as they passed. I saw no self-moving vehicles except for small, city-owned taxicabs and occasional large private vehicles, all of which ran on steam and reeked of wood smoke.

Unexpectedly, I found no restaurants near the hotel. I made a circuit around the entire block, a walk of some thirty minutes, to no avail. A sortie down a side street gave similar results. I checked my guidebook for restaurants. It recommended several places to dine in Deres-Thorm, but neglected to give their addresses. I selected one establishment that indicated reasonable prices and approached a stranger.

"Can you tell me where the Three Sages Restaurant is?" I said in Anglic while pointing to the guidebook listing, thinking that would clearly indicate my need.

The man looked at me, then walked away without saying anything. I surmised that he didn't speak Anglic, or didn't know the answer, but was unwilling to say so, or even to shrug.

A second man did much the same thing, but said something like, "*Clogreth dor sodentam. No fegrosty,*" before turning away.

The third stranger took my guidebook, ran his finger up and down the page, read it carefully, then spat on it, slammed it shut, and handed it to me with a small bow. *¿Have I offended this man in some way,* I wondered. *If so, then why the little bow? Or is it perhaps Deresthia on Fifty Malapeks a Day that is at fault?* I was dumbfounded. Lazar und Budicroux had recommended it highly.

I asked a fourth man if he spoke Anglic. He nodded. "We all learn it Anglic by school where I boy. Beat us if make mistake, so I neffer not forget." He pulled back a cuff and showed me a scar on his forearm.

Unsympathetically grateful for this stern (if not totally effective) discipline, I asked him for directions to a good restaurant. "Ah. Yes. Good restaurant. I show you." He took off, walking rapidly, turning this way and that, occasionally stopping to peer down all the cross streets at an intersection. "This way!" he'd say, pointing, then he'd dart ahead of me down another street.

I was tempted to turn around and go back to the hotel. But I didn't want to offend this Good Samaritan by simply running away from him. What would he think? And by the time I'd made up my mind to return to Hotel Indigo, I was no longer sure in which direction it lay.

We met fewer and fewer people. The streets grew narrower and narrower, the architecture more ancient. In one place, I stretched out my arms to see if I could touch the buildings on both sides at the same time. I could. I felt as if the city were closing in on me. I took a deep breath and kept moving, hoping my claustrophobia wouldn't take over.

A TRUE MAP OF THE CITY

At last, my guide stopped in an alleyway. "Here. Is wonderful restaurant." He pointed. An ornate sign above the door of the nearest establishment said, in Anglic, more or less: "Inn Commodious. Fine Foodings since 1201 AFD."

The place looked neat and well-maintained, with flowers in planter boxes below the windows and colorful frescoes around the entrance. I offered my guide a tip, but he quickly held up a hand, shook his head, and departed. Starved after over twenty four hours with nothing to eat, I approached "Inn Commodious" and pulled on the door handle with the expectation that it would open. But no. It was locked. I pushed and pulled on the door again several times, illogically, and then rapped gently. No one came. I knocked louder. Eventually, I pounded on the door, with the same result.

I walked up and down the narrow alley, searching for any place bearing the Deresthok word for "restaurant," or something close to it. I wasn't sure of the urban word, but hoped that it was similar to the rural version, or that a restaurant would at least look like one, even in Deres-Thorm. There was nothing.

Frustrated, I started to return to Hotel Indigo. At the second intersection after the alley, I realized I had no idea which way to turn. I was lost. I looked for a taxicab, but there were few vehicles on the streets in this part of the city, and none of them were taxicabs.

Nor were there any pedestrians to ask for directions, either, so I went back to Inn Commodious and checked the window for a listing of their hours. There was nothing posted there but a small, sun-faded Anglic menu, whose delights included "Stuffed Sylvanian Mushroom with Russian Caviar," "Fillet of Adriatic Sole in Butter Sauce with Caper," and "Thuringian Cherry Tart with Brandy."

As I read the menu, salivating, a man in a black suit and Roman collar accosted me. "You there! Why do you loiter here? Why are you spying in the windows of this establishment?"

Chapter Three

The question surprised me, particularly coming from a priest speaking Anglic. I guessed that the fellow recognized me as Albionian by my garb—a blue blazer and dark grey trousers tailored in the manner of my country. I had no reason to fear him, so I answered easily, "I'm just checking to see when they open."

He frowned. "And where does it say that?" He ostentatiously scanned the window.

"It doesn't."

He stared at me through narrowed eyes. "How can you check something that isn't there?"

"I was looking for a notice giving their hours, but there is none." I waved my hands in explication. They trembled ever so slightly.

The man nodded, apparently satisfied. "I am," he said, "Monsignor Pokska." He withdrew an identification card from his pocket and held it in front of my nose. According to the card, Pokska was a policeman. Monsignor, it seems, is a high rank in Deresthian law en-

A TRUE MAP OF THE CITY

forcement, a fact not mentioned in my guidebook. "Let me see your papers," he added.

His Anglic was impeccable, the best of anyone I'd met so far in Deres-Thorm. I was, once again, filled with gratitude for their early discipline in Anglic instruction. I took out my visa and handed it to him.

"¿Where are you staying," he said, examining the document closely.

"Hotel Indigo." I relaxed a bit.

"Do you have some proof of that? A key? A room card? Anything?"

"No . . . " Everything else, my luggage, room card and key, and my passport, were back at the hotel. I had only my visa, I realized with some uneasiness.

He kept my visa and motioned me to follow him. For the first few blocks, I felt a sense of relief. At last I'd found someone who could understand me, who was helping me get back to the hotel. I only gradually became aware of the expressions of people we encountered: fearful looks, furtive glances at the policeman, then pitying ones in my direction. I gathered they thought he was arresting me. At first, I smiled reassuringly at them or nodded confidently. As we walked farther and farther, my confidence faded.

Pokska halted in front of a grey stone building. It was then that I realized he was not taking me back to my hotel. He had brought me to the police station. *Well*, I thought, *now I'll have to wait for an hour or so while they examine my visa, or call the hotel, or whatever it is they normally do. I hope the waiting room isn't a small one.* I tensed up at the idea.

The policeman hustled me inside without speaking and took me through a lobby and then immediately down two flights of stairs. At the basement level, he led me along a corridor, then opened what I took for a broom closet, at first. The tiny door led to a narrow stairway lit by electric lamps. My claustrophobia made me hesitate, but Pokska grasped my shoulder and propelled me down the steps just slowly enough that I didn't fall. I could hear his boots stomping at my heels, the sound echoing back up at us from the walls of the corridor below.

We turned right at the bottom and continued to walk until we arrived beside a heavy wooden door on our left. The policeman took down a kerosene lamp from a shelf above the door and lit it. He held the lamp high as he opened the door and pushed me inside.

Save for the circle of lamplight, the room was dark. Mingled odours of mold, smoke, disinfectant, and oil assaulted my nostrils. As my eyes adapted a bit to the light, I noted that the stone walls were tinged with niter congealed from centuries of seepage from the earth above. There were, of course, no windows. I thought for a second that this was a police museum he was showing me for some reason, a special treat for the unsuspecting Albionian tourist.

When my eyes became fully accustomed to the dim light, I saw, in the shadows, torture instruments everywhere. Some were obvious in purpose, others fortunately not. I had time to notice that there was no dust or rust on any of these hideous devices; their oily metal surfaces gleamed in the light of the lamp.

Something swaggered towards us from a dimly lit room beyond. It was human, or had been at one time. Any signs of its original gender had been erased by decades of who knew what perversions. I stiffened in horror, and found the policeman's unyielding hand against the small of my back. This gave me comfort, surprisingly. We, the policeman and I, were of the same species, brothers even, compared to what approached us. The bloated face of the creature was human, yet revealed not the slightest human feeling in its soulless eyes.

I had never gazed into such eyes before, but I knew no mercy lay in their depths.

The policeman stood firm. He said one word, an urban Deresthok term I didn't recognize. The creature stopped and smiled obscenely. I recoiled, once more pressing against Pokska in terror. He said something else, and the creature went away, glancing back at me with that repulsive grin. I don't remember much of the dungeon after that, just running back up the stairs, as fast as my legs would move, with the policeman trudging behind me at a more leisurely pace.

He took me to an interrogation room, where an empty cardboard box sat on the table. "Take everything out of your pockets."

I did so.

"Your watch, too."

I complied, and Pokska took the box and left me. Besides the table, there were two chairs, and, in one corner, a galvanized bucket with an unpleasant odor. I examined the beige walls, the red linoleum floor and the white tile wainscoting. Nothing hung on any of the walls, no posters nor any of the ordinary sort of thing that gets put up in the offices of Albion, not even a clock. I sat at the table.

The door opened and a young man in a priest's cassock entered with a tray. He silently set a cup of hot coffee in front of me. I thanked him earnestly, and he left before it occurred to me to ask whether he had any biscuits.

I took a sip of the coffee. It was so abysmal that, after a minute, I began to doubt my senses. Surely no coffee could be as bad as that. I took another sip, and found it just as terrible as my first impression had told me. I felt tricked.

I waited and wondered what time it was. I paced the length of the room. It measured six paces long by five paces wide. I hummed a few bars of my old school song. I sipped at the coffee. The table was seven hand-widths wide by fifteen long. It had been bolted to the floor. Beneath the bucket, a foot from each wall, lay a floor drain. I finished the coffee and strolled around the table.

The door flew open and Pokska strode in, holding a clipboard and wearing a purple stole, the sort of thing that Romanite priests wear when hearing confessions. He shoved me towards a chair and fired question after question at me while I sat and shook with irrational fright. He was particularly interested in why the reservation at Hotel Indigo had been made in "an assumed name." I had to tell him several times that it was merely a clerical error, a typographical mix-up. He seemed disappointed, in the end.

He then asked me personal questions, questions about my sexual proclivities and practices. Without hesitation, even as I wondered why I did so, I answered them all, to the smallest detail. He then asked me about some sort of organization, one I'd never heard of: The Cult. I could honestly say that the name was unfamiliar.

As soon as I'd said that, I remembered the graffito in the hotel service corridor. I thought it best not to mention this belated recollection. Holding it back, however, cost me dearly in energy. I had to examine every question to see whether it might somehow lead back to what I'd seen on the hotel wall. The questions came faster and faster and soon exhausted me.

Monsignor Pokska finally took me out of the interrogation room and partway down a long hallway, where he opened a thick wooden door, revealing a room no bigger than a closet. My claustrophobia took hold of me, and I instinctively grabbed the door frame with both hands. Pokska delivered a forceful kick to my right buttock, propelling me into the cell. I yelled and fell to the floor, surprised, angry, and in pain. Before I could protest, the door slammed.

There was little light other than what came in through a barred window, high up. As the pain of Pokska's kick subsided, my discomfort from the closeness of the walls grew. I began to tremble in panic. I knelt and leaned against a wall, keeping my weight off my bruised nether cheek. I closed my eyes and tried to imagine I was in an open field of daisies, an exercise that my therapist had taught me. It didn't help. I groaned.

After perhaps a half hour, I heard a noise. Someone was tapping on the window above me. I stood and saw a bearded man peering down at me. He spoke softly, barely audible through the glass. "It's me, my friend. It's Gredor! Did you tell them anything?"

"Who are you? I don't know you,"

"It's all right. They can't hear us."

"I don't know who you are. What's more, I don't care who you are. Go away!"

Gredor pressed his whiskery face to the window. "We can get you released from this place. We have influence in high circles, but it will take a little more time. First you must promise to tell them nothing! You must not betray your comrades! Do you promise to keep our secrets?"

"No. If I knew anything, I'd tell the police at the first opportunity."

He sneered. "Fool! If The Cult doesn't rescue you, you will die in this place, and horribly. Have you met Th'pugga?" He shook a finger towards the subbasement far below us. I remained silent. After what seemed like several more blatant attempts to entrap me, the man cursed and left. I wondered whether I'd done the right thing.

Pokska gave me back my visa and belongings and released me an hour later. As I put on my wrist watch, I noted that it was only 1 p.m. I still had enough time to make my speaking engagement. I was extremely hungry, but didn't want to think of food, only of arriving before the symposium started. I asked Pokska for directions back to Hotel Indigo. He rummaged through his desk and found a wrinkled piece of paper. "Here. Here is a map." He took a fat pencil and drew two circles on the paper before handing it to me. "Now go!" He pointed at the door and intoned, "And sin no more."

I hurried to the lobby, with no intention of "sinning." I was free, and at last I had a map! In seconds, I stood out on the street. I paused to put my things back in my pockets, then examined the map. It was only as large as my two hands placed side by side. It showed the names of just four major streets. Two unlabeled rectangles had been circled. One, presumably, was the police station, the other, Hotel Indigo. The map-maker had put an ornate arrow labeled "Rhem" in the lower left corner. I rotated the map until this corner pointed north and set out towards the hotel, walking as fast as I could. I had just sufficient time to get there, eat a little something, rest for a half hour, get my speech notes, and find the conference room.

Chapter Four

I strode for many minutes without seeing the hotel. Light-headed from lack of nourishment, I worked up the courage to ask a native in Anglic: "Can you direct me to Hotel Indigo?"

He shook his head. "I am not know it."

"What about a taxicab? Do you know where I can find a taxi-cab?"

"Not here. But if you find hotel, there will be cab there."

That wasn't much help. Several other people I stopped gave much the same answers, if they answered at all. Finally, a stranger responded to my first question by pointing behind me, bringing his finger up and over and down in a large arc.

"*Lork! Foddis lork!*" he said, smiling. He took the map from my hand, ostentatiously rotated it 120 degrees and returned it to me. I thanked him and turned around. Evidently, the circle I'd thought marked the police station was the hotel, and vice versa. I had no idea what "*lork*" meant. I walked faster.

Long minutes later, my legs aching, I reached the point where the hotel should be, if the map and my recent directions were correct.

There was nothing there but a park. Had "lork" meant park? Or perhaps south? Or north? I walked all around the park, looking down the side streets for Hotel Indigo and asking people where it could be found. Of those who would pay attention to me, some pointed this way, others that way. Some pointed both ways, first one, then the other, with much incomprehensible jabbering in between. Finally, one woman simply pointed towards a kiosk at the far edge of the park, saying, "Lork!" At last, I had found "lork." Indeed, a sign above the kiosk window read, "Lork."

The man in the kiosk spoke Anglic fairly well. "Hotel Indigo? I have never heard of. Are you sure you wouldn't rather stay at Hotel of North Wind? It's much finer place than all other hotels." He held out a colourful brochure. I'd have been interested, but all my luggage and my papers were at Hotel Indigo, and that was where my meeting was scheduled. I checked my watch. I was going to be at least ten minutes late. The thought depressed me considerably. Still, I could be there in time to perhaps give an abbreviated version of my speech.

I showed the man the map the policeman had given me. He examined it for a long time, turning it first this way, then that. Finally, he shrugged. "I don't know these," he said, pointing to the circled features. "But this, this is Rhem arrow." His stubby finger dimpled the lower left corner of the map.

"North?"

"Southwest, in your language. Roughly speaking."

"Southwest?"

"Yes. Long ago, all directions in Deresthia are relative to old religious place ... building ... uh ... "

"A church? A shrine?"

He nodded. "Yes, a shrine. Shrine called 'Rhem-Soo,' somewhere in mountains of Paradoynya. You understand?"

"I think so, but why—?"

"Doesn't matter. Is not there anymore."

"It isn't?"

"No. Shrine was destroyed long ago when Democratic Egalitarian Party come into power. Leveled to dirt. Graves of monks plowed under. Can't even tell it was there, now. Exact location is lost, but was roughly southwest of Deres-Thorm, hence we have traditional word Rhem still found on many old maps. Rhem, of course, was different direction for every city in Deresthia."

"A southwest arrow on a map? What a silly idea! What civilized country would do anything that crazy!" I regret to say I lost my reserve and loudly insulted the national intelligence, and, indeed, the sanity of Deresthia.

The man shrugged. "This is very old map."

"How old is it?"

"Fifty, perhaps sixty year old."

I pondered this. In theory, a fifty year old map should still work in a city as old as Deres-Thorm. I, however, was beginning to grasp deresthought, though I had yet to learn the term. "Do you have a newer map you could give me?"

"We do not give out map."

"I mean to pay for it, of course."

"We do not sell map."

"What do you do, then?"

"We are allowed to give information. Lork." He raised a digit to point at the sign above us. "But we can take orders for map. Soon as printed, we deliver to you."

"How long will that take?"

"A week, a month. It depend."

"On what?"

"Police must approve all map before printed. Then must approve all application. It takes time. Nothing can be done about it."

"Do you have a recent map I could look at?"

"Not without police permit."

"You people need permits for maps here?"

"Yes, of course."

"But... why?"

"Enemies of Deresthia might use map to plan crimes against the People, then use map to escape."

"But how can I find my way back to my hotel without a map?"

"If you had address..."

I shook my head. "Do you have a phone book?"

"Yes, of course,"

"Well, we could look it up."

He pulled out a very small book, the smallest telephone book I'd seen outside of Gewley Gorge. He flipped through the book forwards and back. "No Hotel Indigo."

"¿How old is that book," I asked.

"Not very. Nine year, ten year, maybe."

"Do you have a newer book?"

"No."

"Why not?"

He shrugged again. "No permit."

"Hotel Indigo is at least ten years old. It must be in that book."

"Is possible. They may have changed name."

"Why would they do that?"

"Police requires all hotels to change names from time to time. Is security precaution. Foreign spies might use hotel to plan crimes against the People."

I hoped my disgust wasn't obvious. "Do you have a telephone?

"No."

"Don't tell me..."

"Yes, we have no permit." He smiled and pointed. "But there is telephone kiosk at other end of park. Cost 100 malapeks per call. Who would you call with telephone?"

"I could call all the hotels in the book and ask if they are Hotel Indigo."

He nodded slowly. "Maybe would work." He shoved the book across to me. There were ten pages of inns, guest houses, and hotels. Dozens of them, perhaps fifty. I couldn't possibly write them all down. The entries included addresses, but had all been crossed out. I enquired why this was, but the man merely indicated that there was some sort of problem with the information.

"I don't suppose I could borrow this book while I make some calls?" I asked.

"You have permit for phone book?"

"No, of course not."

"I didn't think so. But no permit, no phone book. Police would. . . well, you know."

"Is there another book at the telephone kiosk?"

"No. Book might get stolen by people without permit."

"Do you have any change for the telephone?"

"No."

"No permit?"

He smiled. "Is not require permit for change. Just don't have. Sorry." He shrugged.

I had only six 100 malapek coins. I wrote down six of the hotel telephone numbers on the back of my police "map," hoping that one of them was Hotel Indigo or would tell me how to reach it. Then I trudged across the park to the telephone.

§⟆

I returned to the "lork" kiosk twenty minutes later.

"Any luck?" he asked.

"None. The first two hotels said they'd never heard of Hotel Indigo. The third spoke only urban Deresthok and no Anglic. The next number turned out to be the private line of a Monsignor Bilboni—"

"Ah. Yes. Police maintain many counterfeit telephone lines."

"To catch enemies of the People, no doubt."

"No doubt at all." He shook his head and didn't smile.

"The next number has been disconnected. The last number was busy, but the telephone did not return my coin."

"That is a pity. Nothing I can do."

I was depressed to see the sun nearing the tops of the trees at the far edge of the park, above the telephone kiosk. The opening session of the conference was over, by now, and probably my career with it. If I'd been alone, I might have wept.

"¿What about a newspaper," I asked. "Would there be an advertisement for the hotel in the paper?" I added, "Today's paper."

"Yes, quite possibly."

"Well, that's something."

"Do you have permit to buy newspaper?"

"No."

He shrugged. "Then we can't help. Come again tomorrow. We try find your hotel then."

"What about a taxi? The driver would surely know where Hotel Indigo is."

The lork man nodded. "Oh, yes, he would. But taxis only run between the railroad terminal and the hotels."

My stomach complained. "Do you know where can I get something to eat?"

"Sorry. We are closed, now." The man locked up the kiosk, put on a long grey overcoat and walked away without looking back. I wanted help, but was too depressed and light-headed from hunger to know whom to ask.

Chapter Five

I wandered the darkening streets, keeping track of where I was, or thought I was, on the rough grid of the policeman's map, remembering to keep the Rhem arrow pointed southwest. As I passed a waste bin, I saw a newspaper set on top of the debris. I looked up and down the street, saw no one, then grabbed the newspaper and stuffed it under my coat. I became quite anxious, fearing I'd be stopped and searched by a policeman.

I went into a pissoir where I couldn't be observed and opened the newspaper. It consisted of a mere eight pages. Among the few words I could recognize in the headlines were: war, wolves, shortage, ration book, sabotage and winter.

There were no Anglic headlines or advertisements. The urban Deresthok word for "hotel," however, is hotel, and I found an ad for Hotel Ultramarine, with an address (Uslotica Wzy 777).

Surely that hotel would be able to tell me where Hotel Indigo was. I wrote down the address on a tiny scrap of newspaper and stuffed the remainder deep into the pissoir trash can, much to my relief.

I asked a stranger the whereabouts of Uslotica Wzy and he promptly directed me to that avenue. By good fortune, for a change, it lay only four blocks from where I'd found the newspaper. Reaching it, I checked the numbers on the buildings as I walked, and the numbers dropped from 2424 to 1984 to 1622 to 1422 to 808. I was almost there, Uslotica Wzy 777. *Just a few more yards to the hotel. There will be a restaurant. There will be food! There will be a telephone. There must be.*

The next building on the even numbered side of the street was 914, and the one after that, 944. The numbers had started going up again. I backtracked, thinking I must have missed the building. But there was no 777. And nothing resembling a hotel. I stood there for a moment in disbelief.

I asked a stranger where 777 was. He shook his head. "No 777," he said, sweeping his arm in a quick arc. "All gone. No more. *Kai-gai!*"

Had I read the number wrong or written it down incorrectly? I went back and searched for the newspaper I'd thrown away, but the trash had been collected.

Sundown came and a cold wind blew. My heart sank. I'd missed the entire conference. All the money spent getting me to Deres-Thorm has been wasted. All that memorization of Deresthok words and syntax. The wrong words, the wrong syntax. They promised me this meeting was my path to promotion. I was cold and hungry. I thought, *perhaps "Inn Commodious" is opening its doors at this very second. It is warm inside. The dining room lights are on, glistening on the wine glasses and silverware. The aroma of "fine foodings" is wafting out into the little alley: Stuffed Sylvanian mushroom with Russian caviar, fillet of sole in butter sauce with caper, cherry tart with brandy. But where?*

It was hopeless. As the dusk deepened, a few street lights came on. Some burned brightly, some remained dark, others flickered and went out after a few seconds. I walked the lonely streets of Deres-Thorm, only now fully conscious of the city's immense size.

After sundown, I encountered two men on a corner. They had a ladder and were taking down the street sign, "Eipriano Wzy," by the light of a flickering lamp, in order to replace it with another reading, "Mesilotka Ssy." A horse-drawn wagon nearby held dozens of these same signs, some old and faded, some brand new. The men smiled and waved at me.

I waved back and stopped beside the ladder. "What are you doing?" I asked in rural Deresthok, knowing that I must sound like an utter bumpkin, assuming I could be understood at all.

"We rename this street," the man on the ladder replied in the same dialect. "When we get done, we start on another street." The second man pointed towards their next worksite.

"But why do you rename the street?"

They laughed. The man holding the ladder said, "Is the law. Change street name every year or two,"

"But why?"

They both shrugged. "Is the law."

"Do either of you know where Hotel Indigo is located?"

They shrugged again. The man on the ladder stared off in the distance, then turned to me and said, "You could ask Rela." The other man smiled and nodded.

"And who is Rela?"

"Bad girl. Know all about hotels." The ladder holder laughed and reciprocated his pelvis suggestively. The other man grasped the signpost like a lover, his eyes rolled upward as the ladder shook beneath him.

"And where may I find her?"

The man affixing the sign looked down at me. "She comes!"

"She comes?"

"Yes." He pointed down the street.

Far off, barely visible, a woman approached in the lamplights. When she reached us, I could see she was a bit heavy, but with nice features. She smiled at the men and stared at me. I asked her the whereabouts of Hotel Indigo.

"Why you want know?"

"I'm staying there."

"Then you should know where it at."

"I'm lost."

She looked up at the new street sign, now being polished with the man's soiled sleeve. "Cost you two thousand malapek."

That was a considerable amount of money, but I didn't haggle. I pulled out my wallet and extracted the correct currency. I put it in my side pocket. "Very well. I'll pay you when we get there."

"Half now, please," she insisted.

I gave her a thousand malapeks, and she turned and walked away. I followed for a little while, but felt odd and finally sped up and walked beside her. We didn't speak.

I had a vague expectation that we would reach the hotel in perhaps fifteen or twenty minutes. I was mistaken. I was growing very tired. My legs cramped and my shoes hurt. After almost forty minutes, I realized we were approaching the railway station. I knew this could not be right; Hotel Indigo was nowhere near the station.

"Wait," I said. "The hotel is not this way."

My guide stopped and turned to me, frowning. "You so smart? You know where is hotel?"

I was becoming angry. "No, but I know where is not hotel, and here is not where hotel is!"

She shrugged. "Is right around corner." She resumed walking. I followed, feeling foolish. Why was I following her, when I knew the hotel couldn't be anywhere near here?

She turned several corners, then stopped suddenly. "Here," she said. "Here is Hotel Indigo!"

31

We were standing in front of a small, grey stone building, with nothing to distinguish it from its neighbours except a small plaque beside the door, beneath an overhead light fixture. The plaque read "Hotel Umbria."

I shook my finger at the plaque. "Does that say 'Hotel Indigo?'"

"No. You think I stupid or something? Of course it not say 'Hotel Indigo.' Plaque, it may say 'Hotel Umbria,' but beneath plaque is Hotel Indigo. I be here many time for screw . . . " She paused. " . . . in my professional capacity." She smirked.

"This is not my hotel! I am staying at the real Hotel Indigo. A big hotel. Ten times as big as this. Twenty times as big."

She was no longer smiling. "You say 'Hotel Indigo.' I bring you Hotel Indigo." She gestured two-handed at the grey building. "Pay me now."

"This is not Hotel Indigo! I won't pay you. I could go to the station from here and get a taxi for less than that. In fact, you should give me back the thousand malapeks I already gave you."

Screaming, she launched herself at me in a frenzy, taking me completely by surprise. She scratched my face and my hands, then kicked my shins and tore at my suit, trying to knock me off my feet. I feared for my life if I should fall. I defended myself as best I could, backing away until I was against the facade of Hotel Umbria.

Her screams attracted the attention of hotel guests. I heard windows open above us and people shouting. I was relieved to know that my plight was known. Surely someone would come out and rescue me from this madwoman.

It seemed forever before a man in a black suit came out of the hotel. "*Dresto!*" he cried. Rela ended the assault. She stood there, hands at her side, looking at the sidewalk. I turned to thank my rescuer. His truncheon struck me first on the right shoulder, then on the left.

Chapter Four

The man asked me something in urban Deresthok. It sounded like "*Wobit ducas femtoza sloken?*" I had no idea what it meant. Then he hit me on top of my head, and I collapsed to my knees. He repeated his question. I promised myself to kill this man at the first opportunity, if I survived. I had never thought anything like that in my entire life.

The beating continued. I was dimly aware of Rela standing there, watching it all, expressionless. I attempted to tell the man that it was she who had attacked me, but my Anglic and rural Deresthok supplications, punctuated by cries of pain, failed to penetrate his policeman's mind. At last, he stopped.

Rela said something. He asked her a question. She replied at some length.

The policeman turned to me and spoke in bad Anglic. "You give it money this woman come here hotel?" He pointed at Rela.

"Yes," I said. Even in my injured state I realized immediately that this was open to unfortunate interpretations. "I asked her to find my hotel. This isn't it."

Rela and the policeman exchanged words.

"How much you give her?" he asked me.

"To find the hotel, I gave her a thousand malapeks."

Still looking at me, he held out his hand toward Rela, who put the thousand malapek bill in it. "You hired prostitute to go to hotel with you." This was not a question.

"No, I merely asked her to help me find my hotel, Hotel Indigo. She brought me here, instead."

The policeman looked at the plaque, then at Rela, then at me. "That what all of them say. Come with me." He grasped my lapels and brought me to my feet.

We left Rela standing there in the little circle of light front of the Hotel Umbria. I was perplexed. Surely she should be arrested, too? Was there one law for prostitutes and another for their suspected clients? Evidently so.

The policeman marched me to the police station, the same one I'd been in before. He didn't relieve me of my belongings, but took me directly to an interrogation room in the basement. My thoughts turned frequently to what lay beneath this level—Th'pugga and his...? her...? its...? implements.

§

They took my visa, then left me in the room for a long time. I cautiously fingered my head and found a sizeable bump where I'd been struck. A policeman entered and gave me a cup of coffee, but I suspected it was drugged and didn't drink it. According to my watch, it was nearly midnight. I felt a sense of doom. I put my head down on one arm and tried to sleep. *Someone must believe me*, I thought. This is only a misunderstanding. But my aching head, shoulders, and ribs reminded me that the matter was not so trivial.

Someone swatted my head right on the baton bump, waking me painfully. Monsignor Pokska sat on the other side of the table, wearing his purple stole and holding a file folder. "You again," he said.

"I'm afraid so." I held my head in my hands, hoping to stop the throbbing.

He slapped the folder down in front of him. "You are charged with a serious crime. A morals charge, hiring a prostitute. You could go to jail for many years for this."

"I did nothing of the kind. I was lost. Your map, the one you gave me, got me lost. I was trying to find my way back to Hotel Indigo. The young lady offered to show me the way for two thousand malapeks. I gave her half, and she took me to another hotel, not Hotel Indigo. When I refused to pay her the other thousand, she attacked me. Your policeman came and beat me without provocation."

"You have proof of your . . . story?" Pokska asked, his voice dripping with disbelief.

"Well, no . . ."

"What about the other thousand malapeks? You have that?"

"Yes." I withdrew the thousand malapek bill from my pocket and held it up. Pokska snatched it from my hand and put it in his pocket. I stared at him in shock.

"Evidence." He patted the pocket. "Now, tell me the truth, all of it. What perversions did you intend to practice with the young girl, Rela?" He took out a pencil and a notebook.

"None. Just ask her. She'll tell you." I didn't really believe Rela was a reliable witness, but I had nothing else to fall back on.

"Why should we bother the girl? It is you who have been arrested."

"Why wasn't she arrested?"

"It is not illegal for a girl to sell herself, here. Girls of Deresthia are free to make a living however they can. Besides, Rela has a prostitution license from the city of Deres-Thorm."

"Then why is it against the law for me to hire her?" I blurted.

"It isn't. But it's illegal in your country, Albion, to hire a prostitute, is it not?" He pointed a finger at me.

"Yes, but I'm not in my country. I'm in Deresthia."

"I'm glad you have noted that fact. It is also a fact that by Deresthian Democratic Egalitarian Republic law, each non-resident is subject to his own country's laws while in Deresthia. This is only fair." Pokska stabbed the middle of the table with a finger.

"How is this fair?"

"Because a Deresthian citizen must obey all our laws no matter what country he is in. So we expect you to obey all your country's laws, too."

"That doesn't make sense."

"It does once you grasp the underlying concept." Pokska spread his hands and moved them wide apart.

"What concept is that?"

He shrugged. "That the citizen is the property of the State, of course."

I was appalled. "That's not just."

"How would you have it, that the citizen owns the State? Does that make sense? Do you own Albion?"

"No, but—"

"All this is spelled out in the *Book of Obeisance* in your hotel room. It's your fault if you didn't read it." He stood up. "Do you want me to send you downstairs and have Th'pugga explain it to you?"

'No!!"

"Very well." Pokska pushed a pen and a thick stack of papers across the table towards me. "Sign this and we'll let you go."

I reached for the pen. "What is it?"

"Your confession."

"But I'm not guilty of anything.

"Yes, you are! You've already admitted hiring a prostitute."

"But not for prostitution!"

"So you say. Now sign, or I will have you taken down to the subbasement for Th'pugga's amusement."

"But—"

"Th'pugga will teach you a dozen ways to scream you never knew before."

My hands shook, and I fumbled through the document, trying to get to where my signature should go.

I dropped the pen when Pokska slapped the top of my head with his folder again. "You are trying my patience. I didn't say to read it; I said to sign it! Last page, idiot!"

I turned over the entire stack of papers, retrieved the pen, and scrawled my name on last page. I couldn't recognize my own signature, it was so shaky.

Pokska grabbed up the "confession" and stalked to the door.

"But—"

"Shut up, criminal!" He left.

A little later, two policemen got me and hustled me down a long corridor into another tiny cell, one I'd not been in before. Judging by the length of the corridor, they had plenty of cells. I waited in the dark, writhing in cramped, claustrophobic terror.

§

Pokska woke me. "Get up."

I didn't know where I was, at first. "What are you going to do to me?"

"Get up!" he roared.

I rose as quickly as I could.

"Give me all your money."

I handed over all my coins and currency. Pokska counted it, a bit more than five thousand malapeks, then handed back a fifty malapek coin. "I have ordered you expelled from Deresthia. You are to leave this country immediately. You won't be needing this." He waved the wad of bills.

"My bags are at the hotel . . . "

"We will take you back to the hotel to get your bags, then you leave right away."

Pokska had two men escort me to the front of the police station. They took me outside into mid-day sunlight, then put me in a horse-drawn vehicle and drove me back to Hotel Indigo. The right Hotel Indigo. The sight cheered me a little.

I went inside, still terrified, but relieved to be back in familiar surroundings. The carpet, the front desk, even the surly clerk, all these things seemed good. I approached the clerk and managed to smile at him. He did not smile back. "I need the key to my room," I told him.

"What number?"

I stared at him. "Number? I . . . I . . . don't remember."

He looked at me. "You sure you staying here?"

"Yes." Suddenly I felt a wave of vertigo. *What if this is no longer Hotel Indigo. What if the name has been changed?* "This is Hotel Indigo, isn't it?"

"Yes, is Hotel Indigo. Your name?"

"Oh, yes, my name . . . " *What if I can't remember my name? What if I've forgotten that, too?* "Blassingame! Horus Blassingame!"

"We have no Blassingame here."

Chapter Seven

The hotel hotel clerk repeated, "Is no Blassingame staying at this place."

"Yes, there is."

"You are mistaken."

"Wait. You had my reservation wrong. You had me down as Plastingane. Horace Plastingane."

"Is no Plastingane here, either."

"But you must have me here. I stayed here last night . . ."

"No, last night you were not here. I would know."

"But I was here the night before . . ."

He nodded. "Yes, you were here then."

I almost fainted with relief. I'd thought I was going mad. "Yes. Yes. My bags are in my room. You must remember what room I was in—"

"We don't have your bags. You no longer welcome at Hotel Indigo."

"But . . . why?"

He sneered at me, his eyes lit with fury. "Because you are degenerate! You filthy rapist, you try to rape innocent Deresthian girl, a wirgin."

"Rela? She's no virgin; she's a . . . a whore." I'd never spoken that word before in my life.

"Swine!" The clerk swept his hand across the counter and slapped my face so hard I saw lights flash at the corners of both my eyes.

I was shocked. I stepped back and managed to blurt out, "I never touched her!"

"Out! Get out now, or I call police."

"What about my passport?"

He sneered and reached beneath the desk. I took another step backwards, thinking he might have a weapon there. But instead, he took out a large ashtray containing a small heap of ashes. "Here you passport, you perwert!"

Was that really the remains of my passport? There was no way to tell. I left. I went back out into bright sunshine, but in my mind, it was black as night. *I am ruined. My career is over. I've been arrested, robbed, insulted, beaten, and now thrown out of my hotel. My luggage has apparently been appropriated. I have only fifty malapeks. And I am being deported. Without my passport.*

I certainly didn't mind leaving. Despite the shame that awaited me in Albion, I wanted to go home more than anything in the world. But how far would my fifty malapeks take me? I tried to remember the distance to the nearest border, but couldn't. I looked in my guidebook and found, belatedly, that its overall map of Deresthia had been neatly cut out at some point while I was in police custody.

Several steam-driven taxis were lined up at the kerb, but I was certain that I didn't have enough money for both cab fare and a train ticket. I'd have to walk to the depot. I asked a passerby where it could be found, in both Anglic and rural Deresthok, but he didn't understand. My frustration grew by the minute.

I walked beside the hotel, asking people for directions to the station. They either shrugged or pointed in differing directions or rattled off something in the urban dialect. Halfway around the block, I saw my luggage stacked up beside a trash bin on a loading dock. This cheered me momentarily, until I examined the cases. Empty. All my possessions were gone. Almost. From an inconspicuous pocket inside one bag, I retrieved a handkerchief and my shaving kit, with its little round soap container and shiny straight razor still in the leather pouch. Whatever happened, I would at least not look unkempt. In my gnawing hunger, I considered eating the soap, but decided that would be a bad idea. I put these precious remnants of my past self in my pockets, then trudged further around the block.

I was almost back to the main entrance of Hotel Indigo. As I turned another corner, I encountered a group of ugly men carrying clubs and ropes. They seemed as surprised as I was. One of them saw me, pointed, and yelled, "There he is! That's him!"

I didn't wait to see what they had in mind, but hared off the way I'd come. They pursued me for almost half a league. My criquét days of long ago still bore fruit. I'd acquired a bit of a paunch, but my leg muscles hadn't forgotten how to carry me at a reasonable pace. Unfortunately, my feet had lost their calluses, and the "reasonable pace" became slower and slower. I looked behind me and saw that the last few of my pursuers had stopped to pant and shake their fists at me.

I turned at the very next corner to remove myself from their sight, in case they found a second wind. I saw immediately that I'd run into a short delivery alley, closed off at the far end. I dared not run back out again. I staggered along on aching feet, searching for a loading dock, an open door, a window, anything. I imagined the mob reforming behind me, poised to respond to the rallying cry of "There he is, now!"

    I found no unlocked doors. At the end of the alley, there was a sort of small hatch consisting of a hinged piece of laminated wood held in place with a rusty hasp. I opened it. The stench of garbage emanating from the opening almost knocked me down. I imagined once more a mob gathering behind me and quickly crawled into the dark, odorous hole.

Chapter Eight

I found myself in a narrow garbage chute. Ducking to avoid hitting my injured head on the low ceiling, I pulled the hatch closed behind me and wedged it into position as best I could. Perhaps I can wait here until nightfall, then find my way to the train station. Will my last fifty malapeks get me across the border into Congrezia? I certainly hoped so. I sat in the darkened passageway, covered my nose with my hand to block the smell, and settled in for a long wait.

I froze in terror as someone began scrabbling at the wooden door, apparently trying to get in. I half stood and crept further into the building as silently as I could. I heard the plywood hatch fall outward. A second later, I rammed my head into a door at the end of the chute. The pain sent me to my knees, but I dared not cry out. I opened the door and found that it led into a faintly lit hallway where I could stand up. I sprinted along, turning right or left, heedless of my increasing disorientation. I heard, or imagined I heard, someone running behind me. Only after a minute of this did I realize I might not be able to find my way out again.

My feet are surely bleeding, by now, I thought. *I probably have blisters on my blisters.* My head, my bruised sides and buttock ached; each breath was agony. I no longer heard footsteps behind me, so I paused to try several of the doors that opened off this corridor, but they were all locked. I hurried on, turned another corner, and ran right into a man in an overcoat.

"*¿Gnosko borovik senuba zilkas,*" he hissed at me.

"I don't speak your language," I whispered. "Do you speak Anglic?"

"Yes." He pulled out a large, ancient revolver and pointed it at me. "What you name?" Even in the faint light, I could see the gun was loaded.

I thought quickly. "Albertus Magnus," I replied.

He lowered the weapon. "You have password?"

"Why do I need a password? "

"To attend meeting, of course."

"What meeting? "

"You not know?" He raised the revolver in a shaky hand, his finger on the trigger.

I fought an urge to turn and run. What did that graffito in the hotel corridor say? Oh, yes, the Cult. "Yes, I know. I want to find the Cult meeting."

"Good. Give password."

I took a wild guess. "The Cult soars."

He lowered his weapon again. "That was password last month. You need password for this month."

"I don't know the new password."

I expected him to raise the gun and possibly shoot me. He did neither. After a few seconds, he said, "New password is 'The Cult dance the kazatsky'."

"The Cult dance the kazatsky?"

He put the revolver away. "Come, Albertus Magnus. Meeting this way."

He led me up a stairway, then along a hallway and into a large room with a few dozen people present. It was a theatre, with a curtained stage at the far end, and wooden folding chairs leaning against one wall. Chairs, perhaps thirty in all, had been set up close to the stage. People turned and nodded to me. Friendly faces. I cared not what they were doing here. I only wanted to rest my feet in a safe place and get my breath.

All the chairs were occupied, so I took one from beside the wall to my left. Too tired to lift it, I dragged it into an empty space to the left of the others, set it up, and collapsed onto it, despite my bruised buttock's objection.

The curtains opened, and a man appeared on the stage carrying a small piece of paper. He shouted, "*Brodenkos! Zoromek laboni doobek!!*" Or something similar.

He waved the note and everyone applauded. I did so, too, lest I stand out.

"*Brodenkos! Zoromek alleguzik na numbrekkis!*" More applause.

After a long pause, the speaker introduced another man. While the latter ascended the stage by the stairs at one side, I looked about the room. It was quite dingy. The ceiling had been fancy at one time, but large sections of the plasterwork had fallen off. The chandelier in the centre of the ceiling was dark; four bare light bulbs dangled on woven cords near it. Conduits ran across the ceiling to the four bulbs and down the walls. The door at the back that I'd entered by was now closed. Beside it, a man slouched. He glared at me, so I turned away and pretended to listen to the new speaker launch into his monologue.

After several more speeches, two men wheeled out an apparatus for displaying motion pictures. The operators of this device didn't seem very proficient in its use and lost considerable time arguing about how to set it up. I used the delay to take another look around the room, seeking a way out, should the need arise. This was, after all, Deresthia, a land where alternate plans were advisable.

I noted a second door facing me on my left, not very far from the corner. A crude sign on the door said, "EXIT." I decided that when the lights were turned out for the motion picture, I'd be out that door in an instant. A door on the opposite wall was the closet where the picture projecting device had been obtained. Beneath the stage were three wide doors, no doubt where the folding chairs were normally stored when not in use. Now, the chairs all leaned in long columns, about twenty deep, against the wall to my left. I saw no windows and no other doors. I felt trapped.

A minute later, the motion picture machine began to flutter. The men bumbling around it all smiled and nodded, and a flickering image appeared on the front of one man's shirt. He moved aside and let it fill a screen at the rear of the stage. People applauded, and I heard the man beside the entry door switch off the lights. Darkness.

A grainy, spot-flecked silent film was being shown. On the screen, a man sauntered out of a house, frowning and squinting in bright sunlight. He stood still, swiveled toward the camera, and took off his Homburg to wave it jerkily. Enthusiastic applause erupted from the audience. A few men towards the front began to sing something equally heart-felt. I understood scarcely a word, of course, but the sentiment touched me, somehow.

A second later, I jumped out of my seat and sped in the semi-darkness towards what had seemed to be another exit. I grasped the knob on the left side of the door and gave it a turn, or tried to. This "exit" was locked. I reached up and fumbled along the sill above it, hoping to find a concealed key, but without success. There was a switch beside the door, a plain metal box with conduit coming out the top. I felt atop and under the box, still hoping to find a key. Nothing. I groaned silently in frustration. I wanted to leave, find the train station, and depart this wretched country.

Boom! Boom! Boom! Fists pounded at the entrance. Someone turned off the projector, plunging the room into total darkness.

Chapter Nine

Fists continued to pound on the door. Men shouted and blundered about in the darkened room. Someone bumped into me, rattled the doorknob next to me, cursed, and went away. *Is there another way out—a trapdoor in the stage? A backstage exit? Can I hide in the closet?* I could hear many others struggling to do that very thing. Someone collided with the motion picture apparatus and knocked it over with a loud crash. I thought of the long columns of chairs along the wall beside me.

When the police finally broke open the main door, one of them shouted: "*Nin kopando! Furdlo nin plasick! Nin kopando!*" Then they turned on the lights. The room was chaos. Men wrestled in front of the closet trying to hide therein. Others threw chairs or fought amongst themselves. A dozen truncheon-swinging policemen stormed into the room in clerical clothing.

I didn't waste another second. I flipped the switch beside me, turning off the lights again. I could still see a policeman silhouetted in the doorway, but he probably couldn't see me. As he shouted and tried to find the other switch, I scuttled away from the locked door and crawled between the legs of the nearest line of chairs leaning against the wall. With no little pain from my bruises, I inched my way far enough into the stack to be fully out of sight before the lights came on again.

I was now completely trapped, helpless, and beginning to feel the terrible sensation of being unable to move. The chair legs were tight against my shoulders. If I moved the least bit, I might knock the chairs loose, sending them cascading noisily down onto the floor behind me. To keep from trembling in claustrophobic panic, I cautiously wiggled whatever I safely could—a foot, a hand, my lips.

The noises in the room subsided. I could hear groans and weeping. The police shouted more orders. I tried to breathe quietly, inaudibly, which only increased my anxiety. I closed my eyes and focused on just breathing slowly, only that, not on anything in the room.

"*Gromek! Vobis Blassingame?*" a man yelled. I opened my eyes. That voice was, beyond any doubt, Msgr. Pokska's, and he clearly expected to find me here. I flinched involuntarily and imagined I heard the chairs behind me creak, preparatory to collapsing and revealing my overly snug hiding place. I kept very still.

Pokska shouted several other things, all of them involving my name. Loud noises came from the stage, probably the storage doors being thrown open, I thought. Similar noises erupted from the far corner closet as Pokska's minions threw its contents out into the room, searching for me.

I was all too aware of my precarious situation. Pokska knew, somehow, that I'd entered the room, which was of limited size and had only so many places to search. I was trapped, not daring to move backwards. *¿Why did I make that mad decision to crawl between these chair legs in the first place,* I asked myself. The only reason I'd done it was that it seemed impossible. If I believed it was impossible,

49

surely the police would think so, too, and would fail to seek me within the chairs. That was my logic, at least.

The search went on for minutes that seemed like hours, every second an eternity of expecting the police to discover my hiding place. I remembered my previous arrest by the truncheon-wielding policeman and trembled with fear, despite my efforts to remain still.

At last, all was quiet. The voices of Pokska and his priestly-frocked associates grew fainter, evidently speculating as to where I might have gone. They turned off the lights and left, securing the main door and, from the sound of it, locking it behind them.

I felt that staying in this room was as dangerous as ever. Even a few seconds of deliberation on the part of any of the searchers would make known my hiding place: "¿What about those chairs," they would say. "Did anyone look among those chairs?"

I immediately began squirming my way backwards from among the chairs. I had to pause every inch or two to breathe and wiggle my feet and hands, trying to stave off a claustrophobic paroxysm that would end in a crescendo of collapsing chairs and screaming Blassingame. Have the police already left the building? Has anyone stayed behind? I feared the worst, as is usually the case with me.

I finally freed myself from the stack. I felt my way, staggering in the dark, back to that alleged "exit" near the corner. I checked to see if it were still locked. It was, of course. I summoned my courage and approached the main door, expecting every second to have Pokska fling it open and clutch me. But it was locked, too, though somewhat the worse for having been forced open by the police earlier. I was still a prisoner.

I stumbled about in the darkness. There was considerable clutter, among which I found the moving picture device, still warm, but in pieces. I heard a noise from out in the corridor. *I must hide.*

I staggered toward the stage and guided myself along the front until I reached one of the storage doors. I opened it and rolled inside in a second or two. Pulling the door shut behind me was a challenge, and it took more precious seconds to close it tight.

Just as I did so, someone flung open the main entry and turned on the lights. I heard many booted feet enter the room. There were shouts and curses, and all the chairs came crashing down. *They figured it out! Are they clever enough to look here beneath the stage again? Surely they will, and I will be caught.*

But they didn't. The lights were extinguished, and the room was locked and silent once more. I was not uncomfortable, so I waited where I was for a long, long time. I slept.

§⊷

When I awoke, I listened carefully for a while, then started crawling out from under the stage. As I crept, my right hand brushed against a small metal object. I automatically picked it up and put it between my lips so I could move without encumbrance. But I'd known immediately what it was as soon as I touched it. It was a key.

I got out from under the stage though the same wide door I'd entered by. I closed it and fumbled my way in the dark back to the exit near the corner. The key slipped smoothly into the keyhole in the centre of the knob. I twisted it, unlocking the door. Exulting, I slowly opened the door wide, not sure what lay beyond. I took a tentative step . . .

And my nose immediately and painfully struck a second door, a foot or less from the first. This was Deres-Thorm. I should have known there would be some bizarre security measure involved in something as ordinary as an exit. I had yet to discover exactly how bizarre.

I investigated the second door and found that its knob mechanism was on the right side, instead of the left. It was locked. The lack of detectable hinges told me this door opened outward, away from the first door. I wondered whether the required key might be the same as the one for the first door. I tried to pull the key out of the first door to try it, but it wouldn't come out of the keyhole. It was held in by the mechanism, somehow. I closed and relocked the door, and the key came out quite readily. I could only take out the key if the door was both closed and locked.

I felt the doorknobs on both sides of the first door and discovered that there were keyholes in both knobs, and the inside lock already had a second key in it. It, too, would not come out of the lock. *Perhaps if I stand between the doors and pull the first door closed and lock it, I can then remove the second key from the inner lock. Then I'll have to reach behind me and to my left to insert the key in the lock of the second door to open it. But what if that key doesn't open the second door?* I imagined myself trapped in that space and having an onslaught of claustrophobic hysteria. I cringed at the thought and shuddered so violently that I cried out with pain from my bruised ribs.

Reluctant to commit myself to this madcap process, I took the key and tried it on the main entrance. It didn't fit. The wood around that lock was damaged, so I considered smashing my way out, but the measured tread of someone walking back and forth in the corridor outside eliminated that idea and evoked another: *Will that guard eventually come in and search the room again? He might. He definitely will if he hears me trip over something in the dark.*

I crept cautiously, quietly, back to the corner exit and opened the first door with my key. I backed into in the little space with the first door wide open and pantomimed the necessary contortions to unlock the second door. *If the second key doesn't open it, I can always unlock the first door again . . . can't I? Or is this some fiendish, Democratic Egalitarian Republic trap for enemies of the people?*

Once ready, I put my back against the second door and pulled the first door shut, using my right hand. As soon as I locked that door, the new key came out readily, as expected. Feeling panic approaching, I took several deep breaths. *I must do this.* I tried reaching behind me and to my left to reach the second lock, but there wasn't enough room; my back was touching the door behind me, and it was also impossible to get my right arm past my paunch.

I had a clever idea. If my right hand couldn't reach the second lock, I'd use my left. I raised both arms and passed the key over my head from my right hand to my left. As I did so, I realized: *I'm locked in here, sandwiched between these doors, unable to bend down. If I drop the key, I am a dead man. Worse than a dead man.*

I shuddered and dropped the key.

Chapter Ten

The key was now on the floor somewhere. In this confined space, I could neither squat nor bend to retrieve it. I didn't even know where it was, for certain. I hoped to all the heavens and all the deities ever prayed to that it hadn't bounced out underneath one of the doors.

I cursed my "clever idea" of passing the key from one hand to another. In seconds, I went into a complete panic, screaming, writhing and jumping, pounding on the doors and the jamb, and shrieking for help. I hoped the guard would hear me. I prayed for Msgr. Pokska to appear, with or without Th'pugga, and end this agony.

No one came.

After a long time, I began singing my old school song. It helped a little, and I soon discovered that the obscene alternative lyrics were even more effective. All the boys knew these verses, but only a cheeky few had the audacity to sing them aloud. I was never among those few, nor had I approved to any extent, other than an occasional involuntary titter at the artistry and abandon with which the verses were bellowed. Now I sang them at the top of my lungs, not caring who heard.

It also helped calm me to wiggle in place to the song. While doing this, I felt the key beneath my left shoe, almost touching the door frame on that side. *Can I reach it somehow...?*

I found I could grasp my shoelaces by pulling up my left foot, bending that knee to the right, stretching down to my left. I took off my shoes and stockings in that manner. Then I maneuvered the key with my toes until, after several agonizing minutes, I had it perched atop my left foot. I was now sweating profusely, my song barely a whisper.

Slowly, slowly I raised my foot, trying not to tremble, trying not to think of the possible consequences of dropping the key again. I promptly got a cramp in my left leg, which was at a difficult angle. In agony, I reached down and grabbed the key, left-handed, with my sweaty fingertips.

I straightened up, to my great relief, and paused briefly before continuing. It was hard to get the key straight into the second lock with my left hand. I had to try several times before I felt it align with the keyhole and slide safely in place. I breathed once again and rested for a full minute, wiping the sweat from my hands, before daring to twist the key. If it didn't work...

The key turned halfway, then stuck.

Chapter Eleven

I must admit that I cursed most impiously before frantically jiggling the stuck key, turning it right and left as I reciprocated it. It seemed like forever, but was only seconds until it turned all the way and I heard the lock click. I turned the knob and I pushed against the door with my posterior, more than a little afraid it might be barred on the other side. The door swung wide open, and I crumpled into a dimly lit room, an auditorium identical to the one I'd left.

I lay on the floor, on my back, my arms and legs flung wide, resting from my ordeal for a long time, perhaps an hour, pedaling an imaginary bicycle at times, softly humming the school song. And giggling occasionally.

I retrieved my shoes and stockings, and locked the door I'd entered by, keeping the key. This room led to a corridor illuminated by a streetlight shining through a window at the far end. I listened for footsteps, but heard no one. I carefully trod the stairs barefoot down to the ground floor. I toyed with the idea of going out by way of what was clearly the main entrance.

On contemplating this, I decided it was likely that Pokska would have left one of his minions to watch the front of the building. I explored the first floor for perhaps a quarter hour before following my nose back to the garbage hatch I'd entered by hours before.

I put on my shoes and went outside. I stood in the alley for a while, then walked out onto the now deserted main boulevard. The streetlights here shone bright as day, being of the acetylene type retired long ago in my native Albion. *The better to catch enemies of the People with*, I thought. There were few "People" about, and I took them all to be police spies. No one accosted me, however, and I walked as if I had a perfect right to be here at night, though I was sure the dearth of fellow pedestrians was the result of some sort of curfew.

I had a faint sense that the railway station was off to my right. Tired, I couldn't run if I wanted to, and it was safer to walk, so it took me quite a while to come across a railroad track and follow it to the station.

The station was dark and apparently empty. It was now very late. No Deresthian trains ran at this hour, but a light still glowed in the ticket booth. I approached it warily and was startled when a man sat up, ran a hand across his face, and said hurriedly, "*Huwer dromenko?*" He seemed flustered. Evidently he was supposed to be awake, even at this hour. Now if only he understood Anglic....

"I'd like to leave the country, please," I said in that language.

"You have exit wisa?" He held out a hand.

"Uh, no, but it's quite all right. I'm a citizen of Albion, so that doesn't apply to me ... " I trailed off, waiting for the man's reaction, suppressing an urge to improve my story, which I half believed.

The man nodded. This was apparently acceptable. "You haff passport?"

"It's back at my hotel." I didn't mention that when last seen, it was a pile of ashes.

"You need passport to get ticket."

In my desperation, I told a more blatant lie. "Msgr. Pokska has authorized me to leave without it. In fact, he's *ordered* me to leave without it. He'll be most upset if you don't give me a ticket."

Pokska's name held a certain currency. The man's eyes opened wide, and he said, "Where you want go?"

I knew there was an Albionian embassy at Trebioni, in Congrezia. "Is there a train to Trebioni tonight?"

He shook his head. "No train tonight. Morning train earliest, and that go Slobonici."

Slobonici was also in Congrezia. "That will do. How much?" I felt in my pocket for the fifty malapek coin that Pokska had left me.

He pulled a ticket out of the drawer. "Two hundred malapek."

Two hundred? I was stunned. "I only have fifty."

He put the ticket down and kept a hand over it. "Too bad. Fare is two hundred malapek."

"Haven't you something cheaper? "

He glared at me. "This is not hardware store, where you can get cheaper hammer. This is railway station. Is nothing cheaper."

I pointed at the ticket. "Is that a first class train?"

"Yes, is first class."

"Are there any second class seats."

"A few," he grudged.

"Well, I'll take one of those. I pushed my coin across the counter."

He looked at it and sneered. "Second class is one hundred ten malapek." He pushed the coin back at me.

"Third class?" I put my finger on the coin.

He pursed his lips and shook his head. "Not any."

"Does the train stop anywhere closer?"

"No. No stop until Slobonici. Is Express."

"What about a later train? "

He consulted a schedule on the wall beside him. "We haff it second hour train, go to Petropolis, not so far. Fare is only one hundred malapek."

"What do you have for fifty?"

He glared at me askance and peered closely at the schedule, running a finger down the price column. "Ah! Here is train go at second hour, stop at little willage, Boogdar, right near border. Fifty-fife malapek."

"I just have fifty. Can't you just forget about the extra five? I'll mail it to you from Dinium. I'll give you my wrist watch as security." I pulled back my sleeve.

"This is not pawnshop. Fare is fifty-fife malapek," he grunted. "Third class. Cheapest fare in whole country. Take or not."

"I haven't got fifty-five malapeks."

"Then you haffen't got ticket." He slammed the ticket window shut.

Chapter Twelve

The man shouted, his voice muffled by the closed window, "Not come back without fifty-fife malapek!"

I turned away and wandered the deserted station. Desperate, I actually scanned the floor, looking for loose coins. Deresthia is not exactly a wealthy country, so I had no reason to expect to find even a single coin. Imagine my surprise when I saw a five malapek coin among a pile of debris in a corner. I hastened back to the ticket window and knocked thereon.

The man opened the window, but said nothing.

"I have fifty-five malapeks," I said, putting the coins on the counter.

He put a finger on each coin and pulled them both towards him, then inspected them closely. He shoved the five malapek coin back. "Is no good."

"Why not?"

He pulled a similar coin from his drawer and put it beside mine. "Is wrong face. See?"

The images on the two coins were different.

He pointed at my coin and shook his head, frowning. "Zoromek. No good anymore." He pointed at the other and smiled. "Robelefska! Is good!" He put the good coin back in his drawer and flicked mine into a trash basket by his feet with a *pwang!*

I went away. A complete tour of the building yielded but a lonely one malapek coin, also of the Zoromek face. I felt doomed.

I saw a large bank of wire mesh lockers used for storing luggage. I was tempted, wondering, *Is there money in one of these suitcases?* There was no one else around at this hour, and the far-side lockers weren't visible from the ticket window. I gave in to the temptation. I tried all the locker doors, without success. Then I found a longish hardwood stick in a nearby dust bin and used it to open the hasps of a cheap suitcase in one locker by probing through the wires. It took me an anxious five minutes, during which I constantly feared I'd be discovered, but at last I teased a dark green velvet jacket from within the suitcase. A matching cap fell out along with it.

I gently worked the jacket out through the thumb-width gap beneath the locker door. I found a pair of new Robelefska coins in the left hand pocket, each worth two malapeks. If I could pass off the Zoromek coin on the ticket seller, I had just enough.

I decided to steal the jacket and the cap, too. They were rather flimsy, but new and fashioned in Deresthian style, with black velvet and leather trim in various places for no apparent reason. They would make me less conspicuous and might help fool the ticket seller.

I put my few possessions into the pockets of the stolen jacket. It fit me well. The cap, on the other hand, once I'd freed it from the cage, was over-sized and settled too far down on my head. *All the better for a thief to wear,* I thought.

I threw my old jacket in the dust bin and returned to the ticket window. "Boogdar," I said in a firm, guttural voice, shoving the four coins across the counter. I'd been careful to put Zoromek's face downward. The attendant awoke from his nap, automatically swept the money into his drawer and slid the ticket toward me. I snatched it up, said, "*Splatka*," and turned away. The ticket seller returned to his sleep, apparently without recognizing me.

I made myself as inconspicuous as possible, sitting in a quiet corner to wait for the train, which was scheduled for eight in the morning. One other passenger, a poorly dressed elderly woman, waited for the Boogdar train. About half past seven, a dozen policemen came rushing into the terminal, looking in all directions. *Are they searching for me? No, that can't be; I've been ordered to leave the country. Or has Pokska changed his mind?* I quickly moved close to the woman and attempted to converse, or to appear to do so. She seemed a bucolic sort, so I essayed a few rural Deresthok phrases from my course textbook: "Is fine morning, yes?"

She nodded.

"You are thinking it rain tomorrow?"

She shook her head.

"You speak Albionian?"

She frowned. "I learn in school. I hated it."

"Me too." I smiled.

She smiled back.

We seemed to be together, and the police were, I had reason to believe, looking for a man in Albionian clothing, traveling by himself. They didn't even come near us.

When the train pulled in, I helped the woman carry on her luggage, and the conductor never bothered to ask me for any papers, just my ticket, which he punched and returned to me.

I grew nervous as departure time approached, fearful that the police would check the train. As the slow chuff-chuff-chuff of the steam engine began, I looked out a window and saw the policemen standing in a circle beside the ticket booth, waving their arms and arguing with each other.

We were soon rolling westward, towards the Congrezian border. ¿What awaits me there, I wondered. *Will I be asked to produce the papers I don't have? Will I be interned there until they contact the Albionian embassy?*

I leant my head against the window beside me. I relaxed. I slept.

§⟅

"Boogdar! Boogdar!"

I awoke as the conductor came up the aisle, announcing our stop.

We're almost there, I thought, surprised I hadn't been asked for my papers. *Perhaps,* I thought, *once you show your papers to the ticket seller, you're cleared to cross over. Or maybe the conductor just didn't want to wake me. It has been so easy!*

The train slowed, puffing slower and slower and finally came to a dead halt. The engineer let off a long blast of steam, and everyone got off the train. As I stepped down to the platform, I looked towards the far end of the station, past the locomotive, and there, to my horror, was the border, complete with jackbooted guards, fierce dogs, and a barbed wire gate.

A TRUE MAP OF THE CITY

Chapter Thirteen

In a panic, I foolishly tried to get back on the train, but the conductor stopped me, saying in Anglic, "You cannot reboard without ticket. It is not permitted, *Zemor*."

"But this isn't Boogdar! I must go to Boogdar."

"Yes, is Boogdar. For thousand years, this is Boogdar. Name come from old king of Deresthia, Boogdar the First—"

"But I thought Boogdar was in Congrezia."

"Oh, yes, Zemor, there is in Congrezia, on other side of border, a new Boogdar." The conductor waved both hands. "But this is the authentic one, and this is the one your ticket was good for. If you wanted Congrezia Boogdar, fare is sixty malapek, instead of only fifty-five malapek."

"¿But what can I do," I pleaded.

The conductor stared off into space, patted his lips with his gloved hand, then looked back at me and said, "Why you don't just show your papers and walk across?"

"I don't have any papers."

"Ah. In that case, *Zemor*, you are in deep *hosskaplop*." He threw up his hands and walked away.

I paced the cold, open platform, trying to think of a way to get out of this nightmare of a country. I could come up with nothing better than to saunter towards the border, staring at the locomotive as if curious about some detail of its mechanisms. I began to feel myself slipping into panic, exactly as if shut into a tight space. Despairing, I looked at the border gate. So close. It was wide open. The guards were not paying any attention to me. The dogs were wagging their tails and looking at me...

It's only ten yards. On the other side of that gate, lies safety and freedom. I can go home. If I stay here, Pokska's men may find me and arrest me again. And take me downstairs in the police station...

I found myself running full tilt at the border. The guards didn't move as I approached the gate; they didn't show the least sign of alarm. In my stupid loss of control, I imagined I was going to make it across. At the last second, one of the guards stuck out a pole shaped like a bishop's crozier and caught my ankle. I fell. Hard.

I was taken into the overheated terminal building and put in a cell containing only a chair. I knew I'd probably be here for considerable time, based on past experience in Deresthian police stations.

I was too warm. I removed my coat and draped it over the back of the chair. I then stepped off the cell length and width. Eight shoe-lengths by six shoe lengths. I relaxed and estimated the height of the ceiling at ten shoe-lengths. I examined the door for loose hinges or something I could pry loose to use as a tool. Or a weapon.

I walked around the room, reading the graffiti. The writing was very, very small. A few traces remained of bolder messages that had been almost totally erased.

"The Cult lives!" read one legible graffito.

"The Cult sucks dead wombats," read another.

A third read: "My name was Jan Chryvplik. Remember me. I am dead when you read."

I stopped looking at the graffiti and collapsed onto the chair, trying not to notice the grooves worn into its arms and rungs by ropes.

The door finally opened. Msgr. Pokska stood there, smiling. "So you thought you could escape."

"Escape? It was you who ordered me to leave the country. So I'm leaving." I knew this probably wouldn't be of any help.

"I ordered you out yesterday. This is today, and you are still here. Therefore you are here illegally and must be arrested and punished.

"Without a trial?

He waved a hand dismissively. "Arrested, punished, and tried, I meant to say."

"In that order?"

He hit me twice. Once backhanded, once with his palm. "Silence, fool! This is not a place for jokes."

To conceal my anger, I stayed silent, my face smarting from the blows.

Pokska paced the tiny cell. "You were also seen at a Cult meeting. That is treason and is punishable by hanging."

"May I speak?" I mumbled.

Pokska motioned as if granting me permission to give a valedictory speech.

"I'm not a citizen of your country. How can I be guilty of treason?"

Pokska narrowed his eyes. "Hmm. You are right. Thank you, Blassingame. It's not treason..."

I relaxed slightly.

"... It's espionage. Punishable by slow death." Pokska darted out of the room.

I could hear him giving orders and assumed I was going to be executed on the spot.

§⸫

Despite my fears of immediate death, Pokska took me back to Deres-Thorm on the last train of the day, shackled and manacled. The other passengers in the car did not look at us. I was hungry, but decided not to mention this to Pokska, lest I attract too much of his attention.

It was dark when we reached Deres-Thorm. At the depot, a policeman removed the restraints from my ankles and put me into a too-warm, blue-black, steam-powered van. I wanted to remove my coat, but the manacles prevented that. The van took us into the police station by way of its garage entrance. They placed me in a tiny cell and told me to sit in the chair and wait. For what, I wasn't sure, nor did I ask. After they left, someone turned out the light and the darkness surrounded me.

Actually, being in the dark helped. As long as I couldn't see the walls, I didn't feel claustrophobic. Also, it occurred to me, *compared to being sandwiched between two doors, this place is palatial.* I sat there, imagining myself in a very large room, a ballroom I'd seen once in Dinium, but never danced in, of course. I was still anxious, but comfortable.

After a few minutes, the light came on again. A small peephole in the door opened, and a guard peered in at me for a second. He then entered the cell and removed the manacles. I asked for water, but he refused, then left. I took off my sweat-soaked coat and folded it up. As I placed it under the chair, the light went out again.

I felt certain I would die here, gone without a trace. What will my associates back in Albion think? Will they say something like, "Blassingame? Blassingame—the name's familiar, but I can't place it . . . Oh, yes, of course, that ordinary sort of chap. Whatever became of him? I heard he went on a trip to Deresthia. Never heard a thing, after that. Must have gone native, what?"

About an hour later, the light came on and the peephole opened again. Two cold blue eyes were looking at me. I thought at first it was another guard. Whoever it was stared at me, unblinking. After a minute, I realized it was not a guard. It was Th'pugga. It was my executioner.

Chapter Fourteen

I began to tremble. I turned away from the staring eyes. The light went off after another few seconds.

Time passed slowly. I grew a bit angry at the delay. *Why can't they get it over with? Or is this part of the torture?*

Another guard wearing a biretta came and dragged me out into a drafty, white-walled room, and left me there, alone. The open windows admitted cold night air. I shivered, wishing I'd left my coat on. An elderly guard entered, humming a tune as he put on rubber gloves.

"What are you going to do to me?" I asked.

He shrugged and flexed his fingers, pulling the gloves on tighter. I assumed he didn't speak Anglic. He ogled me up and down several times. *Why is he looking at me like that? Is he measuring me for a rope? A coffin? Or for some hideous torture engine?* He stood in front of me. "Turning around," he ordered, twirling an index finger.

So he does speak Anglic. Would he be open to a bribe? Would he believe me if I promised to send a hundred thousand malapeks back from Albion by the very next post? *Probably not.* I kept silent and turned as ordered.

Patting down my sides and back, he found my guidebook in a hip pocket. "You not need this anymore." He pitched the book into a waste basket. "You homosexual?"

"No!"

"Too bad. You probably not enjoy this." He then searched my person thoroughly. I shall not describe the ordeal except to say that it was most degrading and unnecessarily lengthy. When it was over, I stood there, my face burning, wearing nothing but goosebumps. He motioned to my clothing, which was now piled on the floor. "Dress now," he said, smiling.

I dressed as quickly as I could, while he watched. He then took me back to the cell and locked me in. Before the light was turned off a second later, I saw that my coat was still where I'd placed it, under the chair, undisturbed. To try to get warm, I put it on again in the dark.

Minutes later, the light came on and the cell door burst open. Msgr. Pokska entered with the man in the biretta. "Has he been searched?" Pokska asked him.

The man nodded. But he was wrong. The older guard hadn't examined my coat; he probably didn't even know I had one.

Pokska glared at me. "It's time. Come with me; Th'pugga is waiting."

My mouth was dry. "Please, could I have some water?"

Pokska laughed. "Th'pugga will give you water. Lots and lots of water."

He took my arm and led me down the corridor towards the little narrow stairway to the sub-basement where Th'pugga's torture chamber lay. I realized that once I was in the monster's hands, I was beyond hope. We reached the stairs, which were too narrow for us to walk abreast. Pokska released my arm and let me go ahead of him, grabbing my collar to control me. I found this most offensive. I slipped my right hand, unseen, deep into the coat pocket.

When we reached the bottom of the stairs, Pokska shoved me towards the door of Th'pugga's chamber. I stumbled, caught myself, and stood up just in time for Pokska to reach me again. He slapped me hard on the top of my head and laughed. I deliberately staggered closer to him, as if by accident, then lunged, sweeping my right hand in a broad arc across his throat, slicing into it with my open razor. He grunted with pain and grabbed his neck two-handed, wide-eyed with surprise and terror. Blood spurted from between his fingers and spattered my trousers.

It was pathetic to see. I wanted to help him hold in the blood, but of course, that was not a possibility. His shocked expression dissolved, and his knees buckled, plunging him to the floor, quite dead.

"I . . . I'm sorry," I said, then realized the utter stupidity of saying it. I began to giggle in hysteria. *Shut up, you fool!* I told myself.

My bloody fingers left streaks on Pokska's eyelids as I closed them.

I wiped the razor on his coat and put it back in the pocket of my green jacket. *Where is Th'pugga? Is he waiting behind the heavy door, expecting me to enter with Pokska? How long before he comes out and discovers me here? Seconds?*

I lurched down the corridor, away from Th'pugga's door. At the far end, I found a janitor's closet, where I rinsed my hands and my trousers in the sink. The coat had only a few specks of blood, which I dabbed at with a damp rag. My pants were wet, but they would dry. *How do I get out of this building? And where do I go after that?* But after didn't matter. I would put many as many leagues as possible between me and the monster.

I considered putting Pokska in the closet to conceal what I'd done to him, but decided there was too much blood and too little time. I edged past his body to avoid rudely stepping in the crimson pool that surrounded him. *So much blood....*

I cautiously, silently stepped past Th'pugga's door and climbed the narrow stairs. I opened the door at the top a crack and peered out into the corridor. I saw no one. My watch wasn't working, but I knew it must be late in the evening. I hoped there were fewer policemen around at this hour. I stepped into the hallway and walked toward the front entrance. My feet squished in my shoes, leaving little puddles as I walked. A man in a Roman collar stepped out into the corridor in front of me. He spoke to someone in the room behind him, and fortunately, did not turn and look towards me.

I realized how suspicious I appeared: soggy, smelly civilian clothing, unshaven, and, without doubt, a murderer's guilt written on my face. Any one of those would be reason to apprehend me. I darted into the nearest room and closed the door behind me just before the policeman pivoted and walked in my direction. Had he seen me? I wasn't sure.

The room was a one-man office, quite dim, with only faint light coming through the frosted glass window in the door. I backed into the shadows. The policeman walked right past, facing straight ahead. I was safe... for a while.

I longed for a chance to take my soggy clothes off and dry them, but, after my ordeal with the old guard, being naked in a Deresthian police station would make me feel far too vulnerable. It was then that I noticed a black uniform coat hanging beside the door. It fit well enough, though a bit tight in the chest if fully buttoned, and was much less likely to attract attention than the green velvet jacket. I searched the room for a hat or matching trousers. Nothing.

My own trousers were dark grey, not really black, but they almost matched the uniform coat, now that they were damp. When they dried fully, they might stand out, but I didn't intend to be in the police station when that happened.

I took off my brown shoes and dried my stockings as well as I could with some scrap paper. Ink from a desk pen set darkened the shoes enough to pass for black. After a half hour, I dressed again. I then took a book from the desk and stepped out into the hallway, pretending to read. Of the few men I passed, none challenged me or even spoke to me.

My initial success gave me hope; the terrible razor, now in the pocket of my new black jacket, gave me confidence. I put the book under my arm and strode down the mostly empty hallways, getting ever nearer to the front door. *This place is familiar,* I thought, recognizing a poster on one wall. *I'm getting closer. Yes, the lobby is just around that corner. I'm going to make it!*

But no. The walls and floor of the next room were exactly as I remembered, except there was no doorway to outside. Where it had been was newly plastered over, with fine smears of plaster dust arcing here and there across the linoleum beneath it. This was, after all, the Deres-Thorm police station. They'd moved the entrance.

I was so surprised, I stopped moving—a mistake. Even as I realized I must step along briskly, I found I had attracted attention. A grey-haired official in a well-tailored, medal-bedecked uniform was pointing a finger at me. "*Du!*" he cried.

A TRUE MAP OF THE CITY

Chapter Fifteen

I froze, petrified with fear. *"Mer?"* I asked, pointing to myself, though there were only the two of us in the erstwhile foyer.

"Da, du!" He stepped up to me, grabbed my lapels, and began shaking me.

¿Do I have to cut this one's throat, too, I wondered. I reached slowly towards my pocket, fully prepared to put an end to him. *I hope I don't get blood all over myself again.*

But the man just tugged my lapels into place and buttoned the top button, which I'd left open for comfort. *"Drosko!"* he said, patting my shoulders and looking me over. *"Serr melyor!"*

"Da!" I agreed, coming to full attention and risking another bit of unfamiliar Deresthok. *"Serr melyor!"* I had no idea what that meant, but hoped it didn't mean "ass-hole." I released the razor, took my hand out of my pocket, and saluted in the Deresthian manner, fist to forehead.

The senior policeman smiled and saluted, then continued on his way. As did I, without delay. I strode down the central corridor, hunting for the new location of the main entrance. But my thoughts lingered on something else. I had been going to kill the old chap, who only intended to improve my appearance. I'd have done this with no hesitation, just as I'd dispatched Msgr Pokska. *I am a cold-blooded murderer!*

I was horrified at what I'd done. Yet, at the same time, that was the moment when I first believed I might actually make it safely out of Deresthia.

According to a hallway clock, it was half past the seventeenth hour—the equivalent of almost midnight back home in Albion. I remembered that the late Msgr. Pokska was lying in full sight in the subbasement corridor. It was past time to go. I stole a policeman's folding biretta from a cloakroom and strode to the rear of the building, which was now the front and the site of the new entrance. I left, saluting the drowsy man at the desk as I went.

I walked briskly down deserted streets. A drunken man staggered across my path, saw me in my makeshift police uniform, and hurried away. I was alone. I stood at a six-way intersection, seeing as if for the first time the streets stretching away apparently forever in all directions, into a world of endless possibilities. I unbuttoned my fly and relieved myself where I stood. I exulted in my freedom and determined never to lose it.

I buttoned up and, with considerable effort, focused on the problem ahead of me. Notions of immediate flight nagged at me, but my new-found freedom and the knowledge that I could kill, if necessary, countermanded that impulse. *No, a mad dash for the border will probably result in my being captured and, eventually, killed. I will need papers.*

I took off the folding biretta and put it in a coat pocket to make myself less conspicuous. I left the main street and took a by-way through a maze of factories and small sweatshops. The wisdom of this was almost immediately evident. It was only a few minutes until I heard a troupe of police vehicles, their alarums blaring, dash down

75

the main thoroughfare, going towards the police station. A short while later, another such troupe (or perhaps the same one) ululated back in the other direction. Pokska's corpse had been discovered, I was certain.

Another drunk blundered into my path, as I'd hoped. For a fraction of a second, I considered killing him. But no. Not again. This man's self-administered liquid lobotomy was sufficient protection for me. A single punch sent him to the pavement. I left him unconscious in an alley, propped up with his bottle in his hand, and his papers in *my* hand.

I was now D'zlomotch Glebrovil, a clerk. Very fine. I held up my hands and examined them. Had I ever done so before? I didn't remember. But these murdering hands looked like those of a clerk. *How fortunate that D'zlomotch was not, for example, a brick layer.*

I stopped in a pissoir and straightened my uniform once again. I found my small piece of soap and managed a rather painful shave to remove my two days' growth of beard. I left a stubbly moustache on my lip, enhancing it later with a bit of black vehicle grease from the street. After thus neatening myself, I found a building under renovation and, despite my gnawing hunger, slept in a cozy space well concealed from the street.

As I woke, dawn approached and morning mist filled the streets. I needed money, so I borrowed a crowbar from the construction site, found a public telephone, and emptied it of 100 malapek coins. My pockets bulged more than I liked, but I soon lightened my load of coins at a small store that catered to night workers—mostly street cleaners, milkmen, sign installers, and prostitutes.

I wondered what would happen if I ran into Rela on the street. And what if she were standing closer to the kerb than I? A little shove might be all it would take to propel her in front of an omnibus or a steam phaeton, her just reward for the police beating I'd received. *What am I thinking?* I put the idea out of my head.

I ate as I walked, scheming. The police would be checking all vehicles leaving the city, as well as the train station. I'd be much safer just hiding somewhere for a few days, at least a week. I discarded the notion of returning to any place I'd been. Those were certainly known to the police and would be watched. No, I must find a new place to hide.

I heard a steady drone far ahead of me. As the noise came closer, I saw that it was a half-dozen steam-powered trucks, each covered with dust, apparently just arriving from outlying areas. My stomach clenched. Soldiers filled each vehicle, obviously summoned to reinforce the city police. I knew these men were searching for me, or soon would be. I envisioned the trucks all screeching to a halt right where I stood, surrounding me. I kept walking, and the trucks passed me by.

Next time, I might not be so lucky. *Is there a foreign consulate that will give me sanctuary? Unlikely.* This is Deres-Thorm. Every consulate would, no doubt, be penetrated by the local police, or surrounded by a team of constant watchers, waiting to pounce.

I encountered the morning musicians, those peculiar men in their puce garb, paired off in twos, carrying long rogonhorns slung from akimbo arms. Dawn wasn't far away. Minutes later, those same horns blared out their dissonant greeting to the sun in the ancient Deresthian way. I found it rather amusing.

I wished I'd paid more attention to the information on Deresthia in the guidebook. *Can I find another? Is there some unsuspecting tourist emerging into the misty Deres-Thorm morning?* I put the biretta back on my head.

Chapter Sixteen

Jimson Beffers was stepping out from beneath the awning of Hotel Chartreuse, carrying his attaché case. He blinked in the dawn light, no doubt having been propelled from his bed by the bleating of the rogonists. He reminded me of myself a few days before.

"Du!" I yelled at him. "Let me see your papers!"

His eyes peered at me through his pince nez like a frightened rabbit staring through the wire of its cage. He fumbled in his coat and drew out his visa and hotel receipt. My morning was getting off to a good start.

I relieved Beffers of his visa, along with his hotel receipt, an Albionian identity card, his new (and possibly accurate) map of the city, and his guidebook. I let him give me a substantial bribe, for which I grudgingly returned his hotel receipt.

I then led Beffers on a forced march through the heart of Deres-Thorn, turning right or left on the slightest whim. He was soon disoriented, terrified, and confused. I pushed him towards the railway station with orders to wait there.

Would he stay at the station? I cared little whether he did or not. I had no intention of using his Albionian papers, much preferring the identity card of D'zlomotch Glebrovil.

Besides his guidebook, my interest in Beffers had been his clothing, safely put away in his room at Hotel Chartreuse, Room 361, according to the notation I'd seen on his receipt.

Gaining entry to the hotel was simple. Wearing my policeman's clerical cap, I stalked to the desk, hoping no one would notice that my trousers had by now dried to a charcoal shade. When the clerk appeared, I scanned the rack of keys behind him, then pointed at Number 361 as if at random. My useful Deresthok vocabulary didn't include the word for key, but I held out my hand, and, as expected, the clerk dropped the key in it without question.

The room resembled mine at Hotel Indigo: bed, nightstand, attached loo, free-standing wardrobe, a small writing table and a chair. Dirty gold carpeting covered the floor.

Beffers was close to my size, a fact I'd noted before accosting him outside. I augmented my wardrobe rapidly but cautiously: clean underwear, a pair of black trousers that more closely matched the police jacket, and sturdy, black shoes appropriate for either a policeman or a clerk like D'zlomotch Glebrovil.

I removed all the brass insignia from my uniform jacket and considered getting rid of them, along with the cap. After some thought, I decided I'd feel safer with the ability to change back into a policeman, should the need arise, so the brass went into my left-hand coat pocket. My razor went into the right-hand pocket, ready for emergencies, if needed. Beffers' almost new toothbrush kit was most welcome in an inside pocket. For now, I wore the police biretta.

I thought the Hotel Chartreuse desk clerk might remember me and notice my change of clothes, so I avoided the lobby. Instead, I descended to the hotel restaurant, which held only few early diners taking advantage of a free continental breakfast. Hungry again, I took from the buffet a wedge of cheese, a cup of watery hot chocolate, and several small pastries. I ate quickly, then, unobserved, slipped into the nearby kitchen. There was no one there; lunch was not yet being prepared. I put a sausage in one hip pocket and three cookies in the other. On the way out, I noted four very large, round loaves of bread in the larder. I took one for emergency purposes and wrapped it in paper from the pastry table.

I put the folding hat back in my pocket and took my leave of the hotel by the kitchen door and strode as fast as I dared, putting a half-league between myself and Hotel Chartreuse in less than fifteen minutes, constantly aware that I might be watched. My legs ached. It had been too long since I'd been on a criquét pitch.

I saw ahead of me a cordon across the street. Police and soldiers were checking identity cards of everyone passing. Getting through the barricade would involve considerable risk. I toyed with the idea of turning back the way I'd come, but realized that the police would be looking for exactly that sort of behavior. Sure enough, I saw four men loitering on the near side of the cordon, pretending to read newspapers, their eyes busy watching everyone.

I joined the queue and waited to be permitted through, trying not to look nervous. The guards scanned our identity cards closely. I showed mine, then turned to go. A guard held up his hand and said, "*Guedes dask bolum?*" Frightened, I turned back to face him. I had no idea what he'd said. Did that mean "You're under arrest, filthy swine?" or merely "Where did you get that nice loaf of bread?"

I held a hand up to my ear, as if I were deaf. The policeman plucked the loaf from under my arm. He hefted it, then handed it back to me with a grunt. I, as D'Zlomotch Glebrovil, had made it through the police barricade. As I'd surmised, the real trap was the quartet of men ahead of it, watching for anyone to turn back.

I saw other barriers across intersections to the north and south. *The police are taking Horus Blassingame's liberty very seri-*

ously. What are the chances I can pass four more such cordons safely? Or eight? Or twelve?

I needed a safe place to wait out the search. Glebrovil's identity card would become a liability if Glebrovil himself became sober enough to miss it or drunk enough to attract attention. I wondered if I should have killed him and shoved him into a hole on the construction site. No, best to do as little harm as possible.

But what would be the safest place to hide in Deres-Thorm? Hotel Indigo? Definitely not. Perhaps the Inn Commodious? I didn't think I could find it. The building where the Cult meeting was held? Absolutely not. No, it must be somewhere they'll never think to look for me. The answer was obvious.

A TRUE MAP OF THE CITY

Chapter Seventeen

I found a place in a small park where I could hide in the bushes for a while. I reaffixed the police insignia to the jacket and took the cap from my pocket. I ate some of the bread and discarded the rest in the shrubbery for the birds, then returned to the police station.

It was better than I expected. There were no policemen outside the new entrance, just a few soldiers slouching nearby. Probably none of them were familiar enough with the police staff to recognize an interloper. I put on my uniform hat and strode into the building, flashing Glebrovil's identity card. The man at the entry desk, another soldier, merely glanced at me and grunted, "*Splatka.*"

Even though it was mid-morning, the station was empty except for an occasional soldier. Everyone was apparently out looking for some evil person named Blassingame, or, by now, perhaps Beffers. I started to giggle at that thought and had a hard time avoiding bursting out in manic laughter.

I avoided the far end of the building, where Th'pugga's dungeon was located. I found a store-room just above where the old station entrance had been. This area had now become the back of the building and therefore had little traffic. The store-room held nothing but dusty boxes of records going back twenty or thirty years. I created a long hiding place between the stacks and the back wall. I made a sort of bed there from a few file boxes. There was nothing obvious to show that the room was now inhabited. The frosted glass paned door could be locked from the inside, so I had little fear of being disturbed.

I planned to avoid the streets for a week or so before making a run for the border. Not the nearest border, which might be expected, but the one farthest from Deres-Thorm, Oestryk. I slept during the days. At night, I'd relieve myself, wash and shave rapidly in the nearest loo, then raid the cafeteria for crullers, food scraps, and mediocre coffee from a samovar. I never ventured below the ground floor, for fear of encountering Th'pugga, and I always had my razor with me. To pass the time, I'd study Beffers' guidebook, which contained useful phrases in urban Deresthok, as well as a fold-out map of Deresthia.

§⟡

On the last day of my police station visit, I assembled my gear, ten stale crullers, a few stolen items, and prepared to leave the store-room as soon as the day shift had gone. I'd located a door to the roof and, near it, a fire ladder to the ground, in case there were policemen on guard duty at the main entry. I merely had to wait in the dark a few more minutes, and then I could be away in a trice. I put on my coat and lay down in my hiding place to wait.

A noise. Someone was trying to open the store-room door. I thought it must be a policeman seeking records. I sat up and peeked through a gap in the boxes beside me. Silhouetted in the glass pane, backlit by the corridor light, stood Th'pugga, the most frightening sight I have ever seen. *¿How the devil does the monster know I'm here,* I wondered. I heard the wooden jamb splinter and the door swing open.

I stayed where I was, hoping Th'pugga couldn't find my hiding place. But he oozed into the room, sniffing loudly, clearly seeking me by my scent. I waited until he was standing just the other side of the stacks that hid me. I put my back against the wall and shoved an entire stack on top of him with both my legs. He roared as the boxes buried him. I climbed over the avalanche, jumped into the main aisle, and ran for the door. It was my best chance.

I was almost to the door when a full box of records struck my legs from behind, knocking me down. Th'pugga had freed himself faster than I could have imagined, and his powerful arms soon encircled me and carried me towards the basement stairs. I called for help, even knowing it was of no use. I struggled, but Th'pugga's grip was like iron.

At some point, I lost consciousness. I suspect that the fiend knew a way to cut off the circulation to my head and thus render me senseless before we reached the subbasement. I awoke just as Th'pugga carried me into the darkened torture chamber. He pushed the door shut behind him with a portentous *boom*. It was too late for anyone to help me.

Clutching me by my right wrist, the monster lit a torch one-handed and stuck it into a sconce on the wall. Whatever happened to me here would never be known. This was clearly a place of secret endings.

Th'pugga stripped me naked. I resisted, without success, if only to avoid sinking into despair and missing any brief opportunity to escape. If I could just reach my jacket pocket and the razor, I could escape the torture one way or another.

He dragged me along the rows of fiendish engines. His speech was slurred, almost unintelligible, but he made himself clear, nonetheless. As we passed each device, he indicated from a few words and gestures what its purpose was, with mocking facial expressions and guttural laughter.

We made a full circuit around the room, and Th'pugga was showing me the last of his collection, losing himself in delight as he indicated the intricacies of its operation. I didn't wait any longer, but kicked him in a knee and at the same time twisted my wrist from his grasp. I bolted for the door.

He gave a roar and pursued me. Once again, he was much faster than I'd imagined, and I was barely able to complete my planned manoeuvre without falling into his grasp. Just short of the door, I jumped aside and rolled under the nearest device, a rack. Th'pugga hit the door, rebounded, and bent down to grab me. By then, however, I had scrambled beneath the rack to a spot directly beneath where my coat had been thrown. If I could just reach it and the waiting razor...

Th'pugga reached under the rack. I cowered against the wall, leapt up, and snatched my coat, then squeezed further along the wall. The monster bounded right over the rack towards me. I fell to the floor, fumbling for the coat pocket. He took hold of my ankle, but I jerked it loose. I knew I had only perhaps a second or two to arm myself before he dragged me up and out of my hiding place to a slow and terrible death. I scrabbled at the pocket, desperately trying to retrieve my razor.

Chapter Eighteen

Th'pugga's hand clutched at me, missed, then returned. I freed the razor an instant before he grasped my shoulder and pulled me towards him with a snarl. I flicked the blade open and had it ready just as he dragged me out into the room.

It took many cuts to dispatch Th'pugga. I lost count as we struggled, writhing, punching, and kicking, slipping in his blood. His final scream rattled the obscene implements dangling on the wall beside us.

There was a barrel of water. Although it was intended for quite different purposes than personal hygiene, I used it to clean myself and my favorite possession, the razor, then dressed quickly.

Had Th'pugga's dying shriek alerted those on the floors above? Unlikely. So far, no one had enquired at the torture chamber door. Such screams from this part of the building were the norm. I could understand how Th'pugga's lack of charm meant that he probably received few visitors, poor chap.

By now, it was time for the day shift to leave the building. I decided to retrieve my gear from the file storage room and do likewise immediately. If anyone stopped me to ask questions, I'd give them a terse answer with a small bludgeon from Th'pugga's extensive collection. Fortunately, the two policemen and three soldiers I encountered on the way out of the station showed no such curiosity, and I merely greeted them with a smile or a salute.

§❦

A half-empty produce wagon rolling out of Deres-Thorm in the late afternoon gave me transportation westward, as I had planned. I allowed the farmer to continue to drive the wagon, intending to eject him after we reached the countryside. The man seemed vaguely familiar, somehow. Then asked myself why a farmer's wagon would leave the city with produce still in it. When I asked him that question, he dropped the reins and pulled out a truncheon.

Only then did I recognize him as the policeman who'd beaten me with his club in front of Hotel Umbria. Now, he put up quite a fight, but Th'pugga's bludgeon soon lulled him to sleep. His papers identified him as Msgr. Levodorgu. I took his papers, his knife, and a sack full of produce. He did not object.

We continued west. Near dusk, I rolled the still-unconscious Msgr. Levodorgu off the wagon into a deep ravine. I saluted him as a fellow policeman, of a sort, and kept going in the wagon until it became too dark to travel. I abandoned the wagon and continued on foot.

§❦

I saw no sign of pursuit until late the following morning. I was trudging along the roadside, keeping close to the bushes, when I heard hoof beats. I dove into the underbrush just before a squad of sweaty mounted police passed me, moving very fast. I took a path deep into the forest and slept in a makeshift shelter during the heat of the day.

A TRUE MAP OF THE CITY

Late that afternoon, the valley walls on each side of me converged to a narrow defile. I saw a roadblock ahead, situated such that I had to pass through it to reach the border. I waited until dark, then approached cautiously. They had set up torches across the road and seemed very alert. There was no way around, and I probably wouldn't be able to kill all of them, so I retreated back up the valley, crossed over the northern ridge, and continued west for several hours by the light of the rising moon.

Later, I heard gunshots, but too far off to worry about. Perhaps some trigger-happy soldier imagined he'd found the infamous Horus Blassingame. A pity for whoever it was.

§⚭

By dawn, I'd outflanked the roadblock and reached the foothills of the remote western mountains. There, I found shelter in a cave. I piled brush in front of the opening to better conceal its location and stayed in it for two days.

§⚭

Several times, I saw squads of uniformed men searching the slopes far below me. I was surprised the hunt had reached this remote area. *¿Why this absurd interest in me,* I wondered. *Yes, I killed Msgr. Pokska and his chief torturer in their own police station. And probably Levodorgu, as well. Other than that? Nothing.* I giggled uncontrollably for some time, amused in retrospect by my naughty antics in Deresthia.

§⚭

On the third day, I saw smoke here and there on the horizon. Though I heard gunshots somewhere in the distance, I saw no more searchers. I waited until dark, then proceeded down the slopes toward the border. Beffers' map of Deresthia indicated a small town at Plokogomsk. I aimed to cross into Oestryk just north of there, then wend my way south to Endogenstein and find a telegraph office or an Albionian consulate.

I was tired and, by this time, quite hungry and thirsty again. The anxiety and my travels had taken a toll on my mental acuity. Near dawn, a mist arose from the nearby Gomsk River. Because of all these things, I miscalculated and found myself far south of Plokogomsk just as the sun rose. Worse yet, I had already crossed many fog-shrouded farms on my way and now faced the probability of encountering early risers if I retraced my steps in broad daylight.

I neared a small kiosk in a sort of park. I was surprised to see on all four sides of the structure, large posters bearing my passport photograph. The police had posted a reward for my capture in the amount of 1,000,000 malapeks. I began to laugh at the idea of Horus Blassingame being worth a million malapeks, even as a nuisance. I grew careless.

And so it happened. In a matter of seconds, I found myself encircled by a mob, some on horseback, some afoot, all armed.

Chapter Nineteen

For the sake of these poor citizens who surrounded me, I hoped the reward was for Blassingame alive or dead, for I had no intention of being taken in the former condition, and wouldn't want them cheated out of their reward if I were in the latter.

Thus I thought it best to put up a token fight and die quickly. I drew my razor, displayed it, and held up my bludgeon in the other hand. "All right, come and get me!" I shouted. The throng all cheered. Obviously, they didn't speak Anglic. I shouted the same again in rural Deresthok, and they responded again with more shouts, waving their weapons. Are they that anxious for a fight? Or is my Deresthok that bad?

They held their positions, smiling and chattering. I lowered my arms. Had someone gone to get the police? What were they waiting for? Seconds later, a man arrived on horseback, riding fast. He reined up just outside the circle. He looked vaguely familiar in his Homburg... *Isn't he...? Could he be...?*

Yes! It was the man from the Cult motion picture, the man on the obsolete five malapek coin, Zoromek himself, the one whom everyone had cheered for on the movie screen.

And the crowd yelled even louder now. Zoromek waved to them, and they clustered around him, forgetting about me. I could have slipped across the border in a minute, with any luck at all, but obviously the situation had changed. I stayed where I was, largely because I was too tired to run another tenth of a league.

At last, Zoromek dismounted and approached me, smiling. I threw down my weapons and held out my hand. He grasped it, shook it, then embraced me. The cheers grew even louder. I thought my poor ribs would crack. They certainly ached afterward.

An interpreter was found, and, after a long speech in urban Deresthok by Zoromek, the interpreter turned to me and said, "You, more than person any, give us our freedoms. You are hero of Cult. You bravely infiltrate police station and assassinate Pokska, most evil man in Deresthia. Not content with, you later returning and killing Th'pugga, symbol of terror. With Deresthia free of those two, Cult was able to mount first effective uprising.

"Police fear you so much, they and army go to capital from all over Deresthia to search for you. We kill many who remain here. You come here, police and army pursue you North, South, East, West, and *Rhem*. While they are gone from Deres-Thorm, the Cult strikes! We are victorious!"

§❧

That is the story of my trip to Deres-Thorm. I was anxious to return home, but Zoromek persuaded me to delay my return to Albion long enough to be honoured in Deresthia's great victory celebration. That day, as the rogonhorns blared and the crowds cheered, I stood on the reviewing platform right beside their beloved President.

A TRUE MAP OF THE CITY

As I waved, it occurred to me: *How nice it will be to go back to Albion and tell my friends of this wonderful moment! But whom could I tell? Who would believe me? No one. How pleasant to drink Albionian coffee again. But isn't that often worse than the drugged coffee at the Deres-Thorm police station? How fine simply to be myself again. But who is Horus Blassingame? Who is that repressed, obscure, and eminently forgettable chap?*

Then, for no logical reason, there came to mind the menu of delights at "Inn Commodious." I realized right then that I could never leave Deresthia before, at the very least, sampling the stuffed Sylvanian mushrooms with Russian caviar, the fillet of Adriatic sole in butter sauce with capers, and the Thuringian cherry tart with brandy.

Epilogue

I never returned to Albion. Deresthia has become my home. Zoromek is a gracious and amusing colleague, and my best friend ever. I am very popular here, even after ten years in my official position. If Zoromek should die, Heaven forbid, many would support me for the presidency.

Zoromek and I raised the salaries of all the teachers in Deresthia. Then we saw to it that the schools really teach fluent Anglic, which is now our official language and is spoken everywhere, both city and country. It's hard, now, to tell by their speech who were once the bumpkins and who were the metropolitans. The only people I am not popular with are the thousands formerly paid to change the maps, signs, and address numbers everywhere in Deres-Thorm, constantly. I dismissed all of them during my first week in office. Well, you can't please everyone. Besides, now *I* am Chief of Security in Deresthia, and if they give us any trouble, I still have Th'pugga's toys in my subbasement, oiled and waiting for those motherfuckers.

&ear; KAI-GAI &ear;

A TRUE MAP OF THE CITY

Acknowledgments

Many thanks to the past and present members of the Palos Verdes Library Tuesday Writers' Group, the Vision & Revision Workshop, and the library staff.

Excerpts from our new titles

From *The Perils of Tenirax, Mad Poet of Zaragoza* (2019)
Tenirax Strapped Down

"Wakey-wakey!" a voice called out, full of morning enthusiasm. Tenirax was not of that persuasion, preferring to greet the dawn only once it was well to the west of him.

¿Who is this lout that wakes a man at such an ungodly time of day, he wondered. There seems to be an echo, so I must be home in my little alcove beneath the ruined chapel. But how did this rude oaf get in?

"The Bishop let him in," a little voice said in his mind.

Suddenly remembering where he was, and why, Tenirax sat upright and opened his eyes to the horror that awaited him. There, beside the rack, was Bungorolo, already stripped to the waist and leather-aproned.

The torturer was raking hot coals from an iron scuttle into a large brazier beside the rack, humming a simple tune as he did so. He looked at Tenirax "Come! You must join me." Bungorolo opened the cell door and helped the poet to his feet.

"I'd rather stay in the cell, if you don't mind." Tenirax shivered.

"Nonsense. It's much warmer out here. Have a seat. Warm yourself." The torturer indicated the rack and brazier.

Tenirax hobbled over to the rack and cautiously sat on the edge, expecting at any moment to be grabbed and forcibly strapped in place. He noted Bungorolo's beefy arms, bigger than his own thighs, and estimated how many seconds lay between him and profound agony. Perhaps as few as ten, he thought.

Excerpts from our new titles

From *Sorcerer of Deathbird Mountain* (2019)

Chapter One

Lord Vinifer, Chancellor of the city of Cis Brogundo, scurried along the palace corridor towards King Strogulus's chambers. He was breathing heavily by the time the guard threw open the heavy oak door to admit him, but the frown on his aged face was unrelenting.

He slammed the door behind him. "Sire!" he wheezed before pausing to breathe.

The king was sitting on the edge of his canopied bed, eating breakfast. "Ho, Vinifer. What is it now?" he said, looking up from his tray. "Can't it wait until later?" He looked back at the sausage on his plate.

The tall chancellor leaned down and put both hands on the nearest table to steady himself. Unable to speak from lack of breath, he answered with an emphatic shake of his head.

The king put down his knife and fork and thrust his silver goblet in Vinifer's direction. "Have some mead, Vinifer, and speak."

Vinifer ignored the goblet. He gasped, "It's...it's Zeundrom, Sire! He...he's...gone!"

King Strogulus stood abruptly, spilling his tray. "Zeundrom? Our wizard? Gone? You mean..."

Vinifer nodded. "Dead, Sire, yes." He straightened and adjusted his robes, attempting to regain some dignity.

"You're sure?"

"Perfectly sure. I verified his death myself. He's quite dead, Sire."

Excerpts from our new titles

From *Something Wicked in Ichekaw* (2019)

Chapter One

Sheriff Del Singletary looked across at the Regulator clock on the wall above the gun rack. The brass pendulum was slowly ticking off the last minute before the hour hand touched six. Singletary drew his booted feet off the big oak desk, stood, and rolled up his revolver in its leather gun belt before shoving it into the bottom drawer. He put on his heavy, crimson-and-black checkered hunting jacket and his black Stetson, then bent down by the big front window to turn the sign to CLOSED. "Well, that's enough shit for one day," he said, standing up and stretching to his full six foot four.

A red pickup truck screeched to a halt outside. As it rocked back on its springs, Sheriff Singletary saw a flash. A hole appeared in the window in front of him, and something struck him in the chest like an invisible fist. He staggered, steadied himself, then lunged toward the gun rack, reaching for the nearest lever action Winchester. He could hear the window shatter and more shots being fired, but ignored everything except the pain in his chest and the nearest rifle. As blackness engulfed him, Singletary fell to the gritty, bare wooden floor, dead before the last shard fell from the window pane.

Wyzard Hill Press

About the Author

J Guenther, B.S, M.S. (ChE), studied writing at the University of Southern California, Santa Barbara City College, Ventura College, and Los Angeles Harbor College. He has written 22 works for the stage, three computer books, fifty short stories, and several magazine articles.

His hobbies include playing chess and Scrabble™, wood-working, wood-carving, screenwriting, puzzle creation and puzzle solving. He designs his own book covers just because it's more fun.

J Guenther blogs occasionally at www.JGuentherAuthor.WordPress.com. Drop by to see what's new, leave a comment, and take advantage of any pending offers. Sign up for J's newsletter, too!

A Final Note

I hope you've enjoyed *A True Map of the City.* The first draft was begun and finished in about 25 weeks with the inspiration of the Palos Verdes Library Tuesday Writing Group. I enjoyed writing it, reading it to the group, designing the cover and the interior layout, and getting it ready for publication.

But it's a fact that having written a book is more fun than writing it. And one of the very best parts of having written a book is hearing from the people who enjoyed it! Please let me hear from you.

Better than that, even, is when readers tell other people they liked my book, either by word of mouth or in the form of a review on Amazon or on their favorite book discussion website. Please be one of my angels and post a review. It doesn't have to be very long.

Made in the USA
Coppell, TX
26 June 2023